THE HUNTED

HOW IT STARTED

THE HUNTED

HOW IT STARTED

LEAZA NORMAN

Purple Stone Books
Purplestonebooks.com

PURPLE STONE
Books

Publication date: 6/15/2022
ISBN: 978-1-958758-00-7
Cover Design by: Deranged Doctor Design
Printed in the United States of America

This book is dedicated to everyone that has ever believed in me and to my new fans. Thank you everyone for your support and dedication for my passion of writing.

The First Night

"Who's there?" someone whispered from the darkness, but there wasn't a response. I gazed up into the endless sky where I sat hidden hoping they wouldn't find me. "Hello?" the voice rang out again. I still didn't respond. There was only the sound of rustling leaves that had fallen from the frost-bitten trees that surrounded me.

Leaves crunched under heavy footsteps as they got closer to my position. My breathing slowed dramatically, but my heart raced in my chest. The footsteps stopped right in front of me as a male figure came into view. He looked around as if searching for something, then disappeared quickly.

I let out a sigh of relief and the figure reappeared. He paused for a minute before moving the bush that I was hiding behind.

Our eyes met briefly before I sprang to my feet and ran. He grabbed for me but missed as I desperately tried to get away. His heavy footsteps raced behind me, and they were gaining quickly. I felt his tight grip on my waist and we both hurdled down to the ground.

I screamed and kicked trying to get away from this unknown man. He tried to hold me still in the leaves and stop the screams that were coming from my mouth. After an intense struggle, he ultimately overpowered me.

He straddled over me with all his weight on my hips and my arms firmly pinned to my body by his knees. A strong hand was held tightly over my mouth, and I could barely breathe. Hot tears streamed down my face and soaked the dry soil beneath me.

"Shhh… Shhh…" he said, sternly as he looked around nervously. His gaze fell back to me as I squirmed. Still trying to free myself. He leaned closer to my face and whispered, "I'm not going to hurt you, but you have to be quiet. Ok?"

I nodded my head, and he removed his hand from my mouth. I snatched my face away angrily. "What do you want with me?"

"I heard someone crying and came to help." His voice was calm and kind.

"You heard me?"

"Yes, I heard you. Are you ok?"

"I'd be better if you got off me and left me alone."

He leaned in closer, and the moonlight glistened off his chocolate skin but didn't allow me to see all his features. His hands came up and wiped the sweat and tears from my face gently. I jerked away. "I'm fine."

"Doesn't seem like it to me." He got up and pulled me to my feet.

A streak of light beamed past us in the night sky. We both looked up and watched its trail before it ignited the nearby city. I stepped back in shock. Confused and lost as to what exactly was going on. A few more tears fell from my eyes as I thought of all those innocent people that were affected by the blast. All those innocent lives… Lost.

He grabbed my hand and began running, pulling me in the opposite direction of the blast. A few minutes later I was quickly out of breath and had to stop. He stayed by my side as I tried to catch it. "Hold your hands above your head and pace." he instructed.

I looked at him wearily and did what he said,. My breathing seemed to normalize, and I began to walk away from him. "Hey, where are you going?" he asked catching up with me.

"Away from you, I don't know you and you just fucking tackled me to ask if I was alright. Fuckin psycho."

"I'm sorry about that. I just wanted to make sure you weren't hurt. So much shit is going on... I was just trying to help."

The ground began to shake uncontrollably, and he grabbed my hand before we started running away from its source. "You gotta run faster Sweetheart." His voice echoed off the trees as he kept pulling me along to a destination unknown.

The shaking finally stopped and so did I. I bent over out of breath again as he tried to get me to keep moving. "I gotta stop. My legs are killing me."

"We can't stop. We don't know what's coming next. We gotta get out of here."

I looked up at him, "There is no we and there's nowhere to go. They're everywhere."

"We can't stay here. We have to keep moving."

"I told you, there is no we." I walked off once again, and he followed. "Why are you following me?"

"I wouldn't feel right leaving you alone. Not in this. Not in the middle of nowhere."

Gunshots rang out in the near distance followed by windows shattering and horrified screams. I started running in the opposite direction of where they were coming from which was the same direction as the explosion. Before I knew it, I was basically walking in circles not knowing which direction was safe.

I fell to the ground and started crying. This chaos was too much for me to handle and I thought I had been through some pretty bad shit already. He knelt down beside me and rubbed my back gently trying to soothe me. His hands were thrown off me as I stood back to my feet. My back finally rested up against a tree for I was still unsure of which way to go.

Off in the distance was an engine revving and it was getting closer. As I looked up, out of control headlights were coming directly at me. I froze not knowing which way to go and soon felt a hard tug on my hoodie pull me out the way. We both landed on the soft earth as the car smashed directly into the tree I was resting up against and the horn hounded steadily.

Slowly, I stood to my feet and grabbed my chest to calm my heart that was beating ferociously in it. He got up and walked over to the car and peered in. I followed after him, but he stopped me and turned me around. "Don't." he said, sadly.

I began to get hysterical, "They're dead?" I tried to push past him to get to the car, but he held me back and started gently pushing me away. "Maybe they're still alive. They need our help." He wasn't having it. I began to hit him and get past him, but he held me firmly.

The ground rumbled beneath our feet. The both of us looked to see where the source was coming from only to see the ground collapsing in a straight path directly at us. This time, I grabbed his hoodie and pulled him out the way as we began to run in the opposite direction of the collapsing earth. I felt a tug as we quickly changed directions once we saw another impression coming towards us.

The harsh sound of metal crunching and the loud clashes of glass shattering made us stop and turn around. Our hands came up to our ears to muffle the sounds while we watched, confused and frightened, as the winged terrors trashed the car into pieces. The sound of the horn stopped, and they disappeared back into the ground.

"What the fuck are those things?" I whispered.

"I don't know but let's get the fuck out of here before we're next." He grabbed my hand, and we began to run once again in the never-ending darkness. It engulfed us like the plague that was cast upon us. Unwanted. Unprecedented. Unknown.

"I can't go any further." I yelled out and stopped a few minutes later. "I can't do it. I can't." There was nothing but black as I looked around. The moon was full but was now fully hidden from the smoke from the burning city. My legs had given up on me and I collapsed to the ground. I heaved heavily for air as my lungs burned.

He tried to help me up, but I pushed him off me. "Stop!" I yelled. "I told you I can't go any further. Nothing is around. I'm cold. Tired... Hungry... Scared." My voice trailed off and I felt the warm tears on my face again. "I can't do this." I sniffled.

He walked over to me and lifted me to my feet before my tears were caringly wiped away from him again. I let him. "What's your name?"

"Natalie." I whispered back. "What's yours?"

"Maureese. My friends call me... Called me Mar."

The ground began to shake again, and he started to run, but I didn't move. He tried to grab my hand and pull me, but I shook him off. He came up to me. "What are you doing? We have to get out of here."

"And go where? What's the point of running? We're running in fucking circles. What are we even running from?"

He walked closer to me and stopped. "I don't know about you, but I don't wanna die. I don't wanna be blown up and I damn sure don't want to be torn to shreds by those... things. If that's your plan, then I'll leave you right here, but something tells me that's not what you want to do. So if you want to live and survive, no matter what it takes, take my hand and follow my lead."

The ground began to shake harder. I thought for only a second before grabbing his hand. "That's my girl. Let's go!" We proceeded running.

The tremors subsided a bit once more and I collapsed "I can't go any further."

"I think we can stop for now, try and get some rest." He sat down and relaxed up on a tree close by.

Even though the tremors weren't as intense anymore, the chaos from the gunshots and the screams still rang out all around us. I began to shiver as I laid in a fetal position in the dirt. My hoodie was pulled over my head for added warmth, but it was no use. My teeth began to chatter as the cool air breezed past my wet clothes and skin. The cold was sneaking up on us slowly.

"Are you ok?" he asked.

"I'm fine." I snapped back. "There's nothing you can do for me." I heard him shuffling about behind me.

"Are you cold? I am."

I sat up. "Yes I'm cold." I admitted. "But there's nothing you can do so what difference does it make?"

I heard him get up and walk over to me. "You don't have to be so rude. I don't want to hurt you. You're sitting here playing the tough guy bullshit when I know you're just as scared as I am. I've lost so many people, you wouldn't believe. My five-year-old brother died in my arms. My family... torn apart right in front of me. I'm pretty sure you've seen some fucked up shit too. So please stop with the bullshit."

Tears streamed down my face again just thinking of the horrific things I've seen in the past few hours. My shivering got worse, and my teeth continued to chatter. He moved closer to me and extended his hand out. I paused briefly before I took it and he helped me up to my feet. He sat down and leaned up against the tree before motioning me to sit with him.

I sat between his legs and rested my back up against him. His brawlic arms wrapped tightly around me. "Body heat." he simply said as he held my shivering body. As time passed, I stopped shivering and my muscles could relax more.

"Thank you." I whispered back to him as I reached back and touched his scruffy beard.

"You're welcome. I think we make one hell of a team."

"You think that in an hour's time?"

"You saved my life, I saved yours. I think that qualifies for something."

"You're stretching it."

"You don't have an accent. Where are you from?"

"Jersey. I'm just down here… visiting to say the least. And neither do you. Are you from around here?"

"I lived on Hawkins Street. But… I can't go back there. Not after what those things did to my family." He got quiet and rested his forehead on my shoulder. Soon, I felt his warm tears soak through my layers of clothing before reaching my skin. I rubbed his arm to comfort him, and my eyes started to water. Subconsciously, I grabbed his sleeve and wiped them away. "I'm sorry."

"It's cool." He inhaled deeply.

I hated crying. I always thought that it showed weakness, but mostly, I hated how I felt afterwards. Dry, puffy eyes. Sniffles. It made it hard to focus. Usually, I could fight them. But not this time. Too many overwhelming emotions and thoughts. My mind raced with thoughts ranging from what were these things, to the images I recently viewed, to, what now? Where do we go? How can we recover?

"You wouldn't happen to have a phone on you would you? Mine died." His words interrupted my thoughts.

"I lost mine somewhere running or hiding. One of the two."

"Are you feeling warmer?"

"Yea, much warmer."

"You ready to start walking again? We can't stay out here like this exposed."

I nodded my head and struggled to my feet. I held my hand out to him and attempted to help him up, but my weak muscles were little to no use. We began walking… more or less wandering and found ourselves at the skirts of a busy highway. He stopped at the tree line and looked around.

I came up and wrapped my arm around his in fear. "We aren't staying up here are we?" I looked around too. Most of the cars had stopped and were turned off. People were outside of them walking around, talking, trying to figure out what the holdup was or what was going on. Some were even on the phones talking, I'm assuming to loved ones. And others were crying from the losses they endured.

"No. But I do know where I am now. We have to cross over. I know a shortcut to a plaza."

"Is there food in the plaza? I'm so hungry." I whined.

"There's a small grocery store there." He looked down at me. "Are you ready?"

"As ready as I'm going to be."

He let my arm go and grabbed my hand as we began to walk towards the road. We stepped foot on the asphalt when further up, screams rippled back to us. The ground began to shake. I looked up at him. "It's happening again." My voice flooded with fear. The sound of crunching body parts, screams of pain and panic sprang out of the darkness. Cars began to crunch, glass began to shatter, and a herd of people was coming directly at us.

He tugged on my hand, and we began to run further in the road to the other side. We held each other tightly as we crossed paths with the running herd, hoping to not get separated from one another.

I slowed down in the middle of the chaos and saw more than ten grave diggers coming and snatching people. Pulling them limb from limb. People were falling over and getting trampled. Small children crying. Lost from their parents. Scared and more afraid than I was. I just stood there, frozen in fear observing the turmoil as people swerved around me.

I looked down just as Maureese's hand disappeared out of mine. I looked desperately for his familiar figure to come back. Desperately, I pushed past people trying to make my way to the other side of the road hoping to see him there. Someone grabbed my hoodie and I quickly turned around and was happy at who I saw.

"Don't stop!" he demanded as he continued to lead the way to the other side. "Don't let me go!" The sound of his voice was muffled from the screams and the yells, but I understood him.

We crawled up a steep hill to get away from the road. Hardly anyone followed, but the ones that did stood and watched just as we did. "We have to keep moving!" I whispered to him slightly tugging at his arm, and he followed. The others kept moving too, following our lead.

"Trina! Oh mah gah girl, I'm so scared right now. This shit is too crazy! I miss you so much!" a young woman talked on her phone behind us. "How is everything where you are? Is it just as bad up there?" She paused waiting for a response from the other end. I waited to hear her reaction. "No? Nothing at all? This is crazy... I don't know what to expect..." Her conversation was interrupted by her screams.

I peered over my shoulder to see what she was screaming for. A grave digger had her in its grasps. I turned around fully and grabbed Maureese as I lost my balance and fell to the ground, almost bringing him with me. I scrambled backwards as his eyes focused on what mine did.

"Oh shit!" he yelled, pulling me to my feet. "Oh Shit!" he repeated. "Get up! Get up! Come on!"

"We have to help her!" I shrieked in the hype of the event.

"What?!" he said,, still pulling me back. "There's nothing we can do! Come on!"

I yelled out in frustration and continued to run along behind him. As we ran, the earth began to fall in front of the people running right before us. We came to an immediate halt and looked down deep into the earth as the man in front of us yelled for help.

Maureese dropped to his knees and extended his hand out to him. I heard more screaming and looked down the path and saw another woman in the same demise. She was panicky and flailed her free arm profusely around as I held on to her. She was slipping, and I was too. She was bringing me down with her.

"I got you, but you have to calm down." I shouted as loud as I could, but it didn't work. "Calm the fuck down!" I yelled again, and still she flailed her arm like a lunatic.

My eyes widened as I saw what was coming up behind her. Pure evil. It rose from the ground like Satan himself would rise from hell.

"NATALIE!!!!" Maureese yelled as I felt two sets of hands on my back pulling me up. I tried to hold on to the woman who was still screaming but it was no use. The grave digger from hell got her and tore her to pieces right in front of my eyes. Her blood splattered all on me and it disappeared back into the hell ground it had come from.

I sat there for a minute. My breathing had intensified from complete shock before I shrieked loudly from pure horror. Maureese pulled me back from the big hole in the earth. "Are you alright?" he said,, looking over me thoroughly after he brought me to my feet. "Are you ok?" he repeated.

I still said nothing as I continued screaming. He covered my mouth with his big, strong hand. "SHHH!" he whispered. "We have to keep moving." He let my face go and grabbed my filthy, blood-soaked hand firmly.

"Are you ok?" the man that helped pull me out of the grave asked as he slowly trekked behind us.

"No, I'm not fucking ok." I yelled after a moment. I rubbed my free hand on my bloody sweatshirt trying to clean it off, but it was no use. The smell of copper and death burned my nostrils. "Thanks for helping me." I said trying to calm down a little bit, but my mind still raced about. Adrenaline was still coursing through my veins.

We began walking fast again through the woods. Yells still sprang out all around us as we kept moving. "I let her slip right through my hands." I whined. "I had her, and I let her go."

"There's nothing more you could have done. That was a bold move on your part. Most people would have run." Maureese comforted. "I'm just glad you're alright."

I held his hand tightly as the man's voice in front of us

stopped us. "I can't. I can't leave her behind. I have to go back and get her!"

Maureese and I looked back at him confused. "Get who?" I questioned.

"My fiancé. She's in the hospital in town. I can't leave her there." He walked past us briskly. "I can't do it, I can't do it." he repeated over and over again.

Maureese held out his hand, stopping the man in his tracks. "You can't go back. There's nothing to go back to. You saw what happened. You know what's going on in the city. We have to keep moving away from all that."

"I know, but I would hate myself every waking day if I didn't go back."

"You don't even know if she's there. She may not even be there. Maybe someone else went and got her." I helped try to talk him out of going back.

"I'm all she has, and I can't let her down. She has no family in this area. I brought her out here a few months ago to get a new start." He had his hands over his head in worry and deep thought as he spoke. He paced back and forth as he fought with himself. "I'm responsible for her. I can't leave her there for those things to get her. What kind of person would I be?" he looked at us for guidance. We had none to give. "And plus, without her, I'd be no good. I'm going to take my chances. I can't live without her."

"We can't go with you." Maureese explained. "I'm sorry, we just can't. The risks are too high."

"I understand. It's not your responsibility." the man said, moving away from us.

"Just be safe ok." I added.

He disappeared into the darkness as he yelled, "Thanks."

"Come on." Maureese said, and we continued walking. "It's not too much further."

"You think he will be ok?" I whispered up to him. My hand was still locked in his as we neared another road.

11

"I'm not even sure man. I hope so. I don't wish that shit upon anyone."

He motioned for me to be quiet and stay put as he crept silently ahead. In the distance, there was a lot of glass breaking, people yelling and scrambling around.

"Psst." I heard him signal to me and I went to his side. "There's the store I was talking about but there's too many people near it." I looked down at the dark building. "We have to wait until morning."

"What if it's worse in the morning? What if more people come here?"

"At least we will be able to see them."

"Well, is there another place we can go?"

He thought for a moment. "Down on West Street there are a few run-down Mom-and-Pop shops. Maybe we can find something in there."

"How far?" I asked desperately.

"About a mile, maybe more. Think you can manage?"

"I don't think I have much choice in the matter. Just point me in the right direction."

He grabbed my hand and led the way as we shadowed the street from the woods. Even though the road was desolate from people and cars, we kept quiet and out of site not wanting to attract unwanted company. The cold air breezed past my body that was now wet from my sweat and blood not of my own. I shivered again and huddled close to Maureese. He didn't say a word, just put his solid arm around me trying to keep me warm.

My stomach howled at me. It had been a while since I felt this hungry. I used to feel this way all the time, until I stopped depending on others to look out for me. Took me a while to realize it, but when I did, I was unstoppable.

"How much further?" I asked about a half hour into the walk.

"Hopefully not too much further." he said,.

I looked at him precariously. "What do you mean hopefully? I thought you said you knew where it was. Haven't you been here before?"

"I've been here before. Well, passing by. But I was never walking. I was always driving. I can't even see street signs, it's too damn dark out here."

"You think the lights will be on down there?"

"I highly doubt it. I haven't even seen a streetlight on since the beginning."

We walked for what seemed to be another half hour until we saw a big, shadowed building across the parking lot. The moon light was now visible every now and then through the smoke as we came from out of the wooded area. I was relieved as we walked up to the doors of one of the stores.

He tried to open the door, but it was locked so he broke the glass, unlocked the door and cautiously proceeded in. I started to follow behind him, but he stopped me. "Let me check to see if it's safe."

"I want to go with you."

"Stay here and keep an eye out. You need me, whistle and I'll do the same if I need you."

I pouted and leaned against the threshold of the door as I kept a look out like he asked. A few minutes passed and he touched my shoulder. I jumped from the unexpected touch. "It's ok. It's just me. I don't think anyone has been in here."

"I'm assuming no power either?" I remarked as he helped me walk over the broken glass.

"You assumed right. I think we should stay here for the night. Try and get some sleep. Some rest at least."

"That's fine." I said solemnly.

"What's wrong?"

"Nothing. I'm just really hungry and tired."

He led me over to a corner in the store before he sat down bringing me with him. My back rested up against his as the ground still rumbled beneath us. Chaos still sprang out in the far distance.

"I don't think I'll be able to sleep tonight." I said softly.

"Just try, at least relax your muscles and your mind." He wrapped his arms around me, and I rested my head up against him as I embraced his grasps. I closed my eyes, but every time I did, horrific images danced in my mind. I sat back up and the grip around my torso tightened.

"Are you ok?" he whispered as tears fell from my face. I tried to conceal the anguish that I felt, but somehow, he sensed. "Don't cry sweetheart. It can only get better from here."

"What do you think attracts the grave diggers?"

He chuckled slightly. "That's what you're calling them?"

"That's essentially what they are doing."

Realizing he wasn't going to get much rest either, he sat up. "I don't know. They haven't attacked either one of us. Even as close as we were next to the other girl on the phone. They weren't after us. They went straight for her."

"That's so weird. I mean, I'm not complaining, but that is weird to me."

"Me either. I just feel really bad."

The room fell silent again. The rumbling never stopped. Maureese shifted behind me, making me move with him. I laid my head back on his robust chest once he settled down. With one hand, he played in my tangled hair, while the other was still wrapped tightly around me.

"You feel more relaxed around me now?"

"A little bit."

"I told you I'm not against you. I feel like we're in this bullshit together, like teammates. I won't hurt you."

"But why? Like, you could have taken advantage of me and

did whatever you wanted to me by now." He didn't say anything. He seemed unsure of how to answer that. "I'm just saying is all."

"Well, what good would that do either one of us? That's not me. Never has been me. So stop assuming that. Like… What the fuck?" He was getting madder the more he talked and stopped playing in my hair. He let me go. "Why do you think I'm going to do that to you? Someone do that to you before?" I got quiet. There was a long pause. "Did they?" he repeated in a softer tone. I still said nothing. Just hung my head low. He grabbed me again. "Oh Gah!" He began rocking me gently. "I'm here to listen whenever you want to talk about it."

"Thanks." I said after much time had passed.

The rocking slowly ceased as we both shut our eyes for the night. Much needed rest.

Can We Wait A While

I tried to sit up the next morning, but his arms were still around me tightly. He let me go and asked if I was alright. Once I assured him that I was, he let me go and I stood up to look around the sunlit room. My ass throbbed from being on that hard floor all night as I stretched my tired and sore muscles.

Behind me, I heard him stand to his feet. As I turned around, my eyes grew wide at the person that was behind me. Neither one of us had gotten a clear view of each other last night. Only what the moonlight had allowed us to see, but as the sun kissed his chocolate skin, I couldn't help but to be amazed at what I saw.

He. Was. Handsome. Breathtakingly handsome. The both of us stood there speechless as we admired each other. His light brown eyes danced over me, then he revealed a beautiful white smile. Our eyes locked briefly but I couldn't keep mine on him and I blushed away.

"Well damn." he said, in a low voice breaking the silence.

"What?"

"Nothing." He cleared his throat and glanced around the store just as I did. "What are you looking for?"

"The bathroom. I have to tinkle."

"You have to what?"

"I need to use the restroom." I reworded.

"That's what you call it?" he said, laughing.

"Well what am I supposed to call it?"

"Pssh. Take a piss."

"Oh yea, cuz that's very lady like."

As we spoke, I glanced at him every now and then and blushed. His gaze, however, never seemed to leave my high yellow and now blushing face.

"There's probably one in the back of the store. Come on."

He grabbed my hand and led me to the back where we found one and I proceeded into the grungy space. I turned around to him who was still standing in the doorway.

"Are you going to watch?" I joked.

He smiled and backed out. "No. My fault. I'll leave you be."

The door closed and I used the facilities. I startled myself as I looked in the mirror. Blood, tears and sweat clung to my face. Leaves cluttered in my knotted tresses that wouldn't come out no matter how much I tried to remove them.

My hands were scrubbed free from everything that had collected on them. Next, was my face. Just as I finished, I heard a slight knock at the door, and I opened it to be greeted by Maureese and all his handsomeness.

"Are you alright in here? I have to go too you know."

"Give me one more second." I said closing the door so I could dry my face.

I opened it back up and found him standing in the same spot I had left him in. Slowly and shyly, I walked past him back into the store to look around a little bit.

The small space was filled with handmade items and nick-knacks that were of no use anymore. Trinkets, candle holders, sconces. My stomach roared at me before I heard footsteps walk into the space. I smiled at the thought of who it may be, until the man spoke.

"What are you doing in here? You're trespassing."

My smile faded from my face as I slowly turned around. "I'm sorry, I was looking for a restroom."

"You bust out the windows to my place, only looking for a restroom? You're shittin' me." The man's accent frightened me, but what scared me the most was the big gun he was holding at his side. "You wanna take a piss nigger, you take one outside."

As he advanced towards me, I slowly backed up and bumped into something causing it to fall and shatter into a million pieces on the floor. I wearily looked up at him who was even angrier than before.

"Bet you ain't got no money to pay for it neither ya broke bastard."

My throat constricted and my heart rate increased as he raised the gun up and aimed at me. I held my breath terrified. Everything in me told me to run, move or duck out the way, but I could only stand there paralyzed directly in front of his rifle.

"Jus cuz the world done gon to shit don't mean your coon ass can do whatever you want like break into my place. And ya know what? I can do whatever I want to ya cuz the police ain't here to say otherwise."

He cocked the gun back but lowered it again before he rubbed his chin with his dirty hands and advanced towards me again. The pieces on the floor crunched more as I took a few more steps away from him.

"Then again." A grim smile came upon his face as he looked me up and down like a piece of meat.

Before he could begin his next sentence, Maureese had his arms around his neck and gave it a firm twist causing the man to fall lifeless to the floor. Relief fell over me as he ran up and held me in his arms.

"Are you alright?"

"Yes. I'm fine. Thank you."

He let me go and doubled over. "I can't believe I just did that." His breathing increase and he seemed to be having a panic attack.

I rubbed his back soothingly. "Are you alright?"

"Yea, I'll be alright. Fuck."

His face was soon cradled in my hands as I brought it

18

towards mine and got him to focus on me. No words were spoken as I stared him in the eyes and let mine talk. Soon, he began to calm down.

"Are you sure you're ok? He didn't hurt you?" he asked looking me over.

"I'm fine. He didn't touch me. Thanks to you, I'm alright. Who knows what could have happened."

The rifle the man once held was picked up and examined by Maureese. He put it down and shook his head. "It's not even fuckin loaded. Come on, let's get out of here."

The ground continued to shake as we walked hand in hand to the next store. The trembling seemed to be further off in the distance back towards the city and surrounding neighborhoods. As we walked, the sun beat down on us causing me to, not only burn up, but to make the putrid smell of rotting flesh on my clothes worse.

I slowed down and gagged, but nothing came up. My hoodie was thrown off me and tossed to the side.

"You're going to need that tonight when it gets cold."

"There's no way I'm putting that shit back on." I bent over and gagged again.

He rubbed my back before pulling me along to the next store where we peered inside the dusty windows. It seemed quiet enough inside, but he wanted to double check and be sure. I waited outside until I heard his whistle and proceeded in. The store was a complete mess. Items that were once on the shelves now cluttered the floor and I had to step over them to make my way to where he was.

A rotisserie chicken was in his grasps as he chewed. It was passed over to me and I took a few big bites out of the cooked, cold bird before passing it back. As I swallowed, I could feel the protein and nutrients replenishing my body. We passed it back and forth for a while until it was placed in its original container to be eaten later.

"This place is a mess." I noted the obvious.

"Doesn't mean there isn't something for us to eat in here. I don't want to be in here for any longer than we need to be. Let's get a few bags and grab what we can and get out of here."

After a few bags were grabbed, the both of us quickly went down the aisles grabbing all sorts of canned food items and, although they were easy to grab, they were heavy as shit in our hands.

As we worked, the ground began to tremble beneath our feet once more. This time, it appeared to be really close, and we both froze in place.

"Are they coming back?" I whispered.

"Let's get out of here. We have more than enough for now."

As we were leaving, the ground shook harder again and we ran out and up the steep hill into the tree line. The trembling didn't follow, and we put our bags down in the grass. I rubbed my hands from the pain.

"We need book bags or something. These bags are murder on my hands." I complained.

"There's a camping store down there." he said, pointing and my eyes followed the line of sight but something else caught our eye as we stared down at the grocery store we just came from. A group of five people were heading that way swinging bats and being rowdy.

Before they could enter the store, the dirt beneath them collapsed and grave diggers came up and tore them to shreds. Limbs and body parts were thrown everywhere, and it happened so quickly, no screams were let out. I covered my mouth and watched in horror as this all unfolded before us. Maureese took a few steps back in shock as the grave diggers quickly dove back into the ground.

He looked down at me. "All that time we were in there and nothing. And they didn't even make it to the front door? I don't get it."

My eyes teared up. "I don't get it either. That could have been us."

He held me tight to him. "But it wasn't. We're still here."

"Do we still have to go down there?"

"We need the supplies in that store. It'll have flashlights, blankets, fresh clothes and probably a tent."

"Can we at least wait a while to ensure that it's clear?"

He looked down at me again and nodded in agreeanment. "We can wait. Let's eat something while we do."

My back was pressed up against a tree as I dug around in the bags for something appetizing to eat. Once we found something, he opened the cans and we let the contents roll into our mouths. A small, single rose was placed on my leg after he finished eating and it made me smile.

"When did you get this?" I asked, smelling the beautiful flower.

"In the store. It's not much, but I thought you'd might like it."

"I do. Thank you." I placed it back on my leg and continued to eat. Continued to wait for the trembling to go further in the distance.

Get It Off

An hour had passed and finally, the trembling had relented enough for our comfort and then some. We stood to our feet and cautiously made our way down to the camping store and entered. A putrid smell penetrated my nose causing me to cover up my nose.

"What the fuck is that smell?"

His face screwed up right along with mine. "I have no idea. I'm going this way to make sure no one else is in here. You go that way." He directed me to the left, while he went right.

Up and down I searched the aisles to ensure we were alone in the rather large store but the closer I got to the back wall, the stronger the smell got. As I made my way into the last aisle, I lost my footing and slid but before my face could hit the floor, I caught myself.

The floor was covered in a dark, burgundy slime that now was all over my hands and clothes. I closely examined it from the floor trying to figure out what it was until I looked up and saw a torso in front of me. I gasped. Surprised at the sight of just the torso. No arms, no head, no legs.

I turned to get up and was greeted by the head. The eyes were open and staring directly at me. I let out a horrified scream and tried to get up again but found myself slopping and sliding in the burgundy sludge that I now realized was coagulated blood. It was smeared and splattered everywhere in the aisle, on the shelves and now on my pants and shirt. My sneakers were covered in exposed, decomposing insides.

Over and over again I screamed. Each time I looked in a new direction, there were new body parts in my sight. The stench was horrific and was similar to the smell that was on my hoodie earlier. I began to hyperventilate.

A strong, firm grip on the back of my shirt hoisted me up. "Fuck!" Maureese blurted, nearly falling himself. "Shh. Don't scream." he repeated.

"Get it off. Get it off." I yelled while my hands rubbed up and down on my clothes as I tried to free them from the sludge, but my clothes were just as nasty as my hands were. I was guided over to a clear aisle, and I gagged. I tried to hold down the contents in my stomach, but it was no use. I turned away from him and up it came.

"Aww damn." He stood there for a minute not knowing what to do. "Stay here. I'll be back."

Tears streamed down my face as well as snot as I quickly got undressed and tossed my filthy clothes over to the side and stood there in nothing but my bra and underwear. My pale skin was stained from the blood that had seeped through my clothing.

It didn't take long for him to return, and he tugged at my arm leading me over to a bench where he sat me down and began to clean me up. My face was wiped clean with a fresh shirt before my hands were. A wet wipe was used to help remove the rest of the blood off my skin, but it poorly managed to do so. It was better than nothing.

Another shirt was placed over my head and instantly, warmth fell over my body. He handed me a clean pair of pants that I threw on as well before he pulled me in for a hug.

"You ok? You didn't get hurt?" I shook my head as he slowly and carefully examined me.

"Sorry." I uttered weakly and sniffled.

"No need to be sorry." He stopped and looked around. The building is secure. Stay put, I'll be back."

My stomach felt empty. My throat hurt from screaming. Burned from vomiting. My muscles were sore. Mouth was dry. He came back with water that I quickly guzzled down and socks that warmed my cold toes.

"I would have grabbed some boots for you, but I didn't know your size. They're over there. Come on."

"Can we just... Get what we need and get out of here."

"Of course."

The boots weren't the most fashionable things ever, but it was more than I had and waterproof. They were quickly thrown on and laced up. While I was putting them on, he wandered off to get a few camping bags that he spotted earlier. I made my way over to the clothes section and began pulling a few fresh shirts and sweatpants off the rack by the time he returned.

The clothes were folded military style and packed away in an empty bag.

"Why are you folding it like that?"

"It saves room in the bags."

There was a brief pause as he watched me work. "How are you feeling?"

I looked up at him and blushed a bit. It was something about the way he was looking at me that made me do so. "I'm doing alright. Been better."

He scanned the clothes racks. "I wish they had more colors. I don't want to be walking around like you." he teased.

I looked down at my camouflage shirt then back at him. "Don't be mad you can't rock it how I do."

"I think everyone would be mad if they rocked it how you did."

"Shut up. I'm comfortable. That's all that matters."

"Yea, keep telling yourself that."

"Gah, you're so mean." I said quietly.

Noticing my change in tone, he looked down at me. "Don't be like that. I'm only messing with you. You still cute to me."

I smiled slightly as he grabbed a few clothes for himself and began to strip off his shirt in front of me. I looked at him surprised as he stood there in nothing but his wife-beater.

"What are you doing?" My face unwillingly turned away from him and my hands covered my eyes. But oh how I wanted to get a sneak peek.

"Umm… I'm changing. What does it look like?"

"You could have warned me before you started stripping." I walked up the aisle a little more to give him privacy.

"For what? It's just my chest… You were damn near ass naked a few minutes ago."

"I know but… that was different."

"I'm done now, if that makes you feel any better."

"Yea. It makes me feel a lot better." I turned back and looked at him in his new camouflage shirt. "I thought you had a black one."

"I did. But I thought I'd follow your fashionable trend. Problems?" he asked in a deep voice that gave me chills.

"No. Not at all sir. By all means." I paused and looked at the contours of his snug fitting shirt before turning away from admiring this handsome stranger. He didn't seem to mind my admiration… If he had noticed at all. I continued folding up my new clothes and packing them away in the bag.

"How do you fold the clothes like that?"

"Here, I'll do it. It's not as hard as you may think."

The clothes he held in his hands were handed to me along with some blankets and I started folding and packing as he watched for a while.

"I'm going to see what else we can use. Cool?"

"That's fine. I'll be here."

Once I finished packing, I met him by the lights where we grabbed a few and packed those away as well before heading to the front.

"I found something that may be very useful."

"Like what?"

He didn't respond, just let me see for myself. As we rounded the corner, I saw a large tent by the door.

"It's only temporary until we find something more secure."

The sun was at its peak in the sky as we grabbed batteries of various sizes and a few hunting knife sets that were stuffed in our bags. For a while, he stood there and watched me and for some reason, I didn't seem to mind. When we were done, we headed out into the parking lot with all of our bags and items on our backs or in our hands. Our path was direct as we made our way back into the tree line to where our other supplies were.

No Need to Thank Me

The hike up the ridge was brutal carrying all this stuff in my hands. When we finally made it, I began to load the food in the empty bags, and he soon joined in giving us a total of five full bags plus the tent. I shook my head trying to figure out how the hell we were going to carry all this shit around with us. Maybe we had gotten too much.

I threw one of the bags over my shoulder and it damn near took me down, but he pushed me back to help catch my balance.

"You got it?" he asked.

"I really don't have a choice in the matter do I?" I gruffed and put another one on my shoulder. He sighed and helped take them back off. "What are you doing?"

"Take these, they're lighter. What kind of man would I be to have you carry all the heavy shit?"

He helped me put them on before he put his on and threw the tent over his shoulders. I watched him shyly as he began to walk away. I caught up to him. I was kind of thankful that I had gotten in this predicament with him and not some asshole.

"I hope no one will bother us."

"If there's anyone left." He had a point, but I had to argue with him as we began our trek through the woods.

"There is no way that we are the only surviving people in this area. Of course others will try to take what we have. Especially food."

"All the more reason for us to find something more secure."

He helped catch my balance from struggling a little with my

bags. "We will find something."

"I hope we do too, but I'm not keeping my hopes up."

"There's no question about it. I'm not going through the winter in a tent. We will find something. I promise."

We walked for a long time heading to who knows where. The further we walked into the woods, the less screaming, horns honking, and breaking glass we heard. A peaceful calm came over us.

After several hours, I stopped walking. "I don't think I can go any further." My bags dropped to the soft earth and so did I. The wind was picking up speed, and the sun was now gone past the horizon. "Can we stop here? We don't even know where we are going."

Maureese dropped his bags as well and rubbed his shoulders. "We can stop here."

While he unpacked the tent, I held a flashlight up to aid in his vision. "Thank you."

"No need to thank me. We are a team… Remember."

He chuckled. "Right."

There was still a constant rumbling from the earth below our feet, but I didn't know what the cause of it might have been. We were nowhere near a town, so what was the problem?

Surprisingly, the tent was bigger than I had imagined. The skeleton was done, and the next part was to put the fabric over top of it.

"Is this going to keep us dry? It looks like it's going to rain tonight." I asked rubbing the thin material.

"I don't see why it wouldn't. It's made for outside camping. Grab that end and go that way."

I did as he asked but had no idea what I was doing until he talked me through the process, and I watched what he was doing. Finally, the whole thing was done. Just in time too cuz I was ready to take it down.

"That's it right? We're done?"

"Not quite. I have to put stakes in the ground especially since you said it was going to rain and the wind is already picking up. Also, we have to put something in there to make it comfortable to sleep on."

My face fell as he told me there was more work to do. For some reason, he saw it a bit comical that I thought this.

"How about you go make it comfortable on the inside while I finish up out here."

"I can do that."

Fifteen minutes passed and finally, everything was done. The last thing we had to do was shove all of the bags inside and get in. While he finished up, I began putting everything inside. The last bag was brought in by him and I was glad because my body was burnt out.

His boots were taken off and placed by the entrance next to mine. "What's for dinner?"

The both of us dug around trying to find something that seemed appetizing. He grabbed potato bacon soup while I got a few canned vegetables and fruit. The light inside the tent glowed softly as we ate in silence together.

Soon after we finished and tossed our cans out, the rain began to pour down.

"I'm so glad we're not out in that."

"Do you really think I would have you out in that?" His hands graced my face for a moment.

I shied away. "No."

I laid back on the makeshift cot and he joined me shortly after as we listened to the rain and wind sweep across our swaying tent.

I looked over at him. "Is it comfortable enough for you?"

He returned my gaze. "It's perfect."

Extra covers were thrown over top of me before I yawned and stretched, and he joined me after he turned the lamp off. Even though the covers were a decent thickness, I still shivered a bit from the cold and pressed my back up against his to steal some of his heat.

The thunder cracked loudly and sounded uncomfortably close, so I turned and buried my face in the back of his hoodie. Unexpectedly, he turned and faced me and held me tightly to him as he played in my tangled hair.

"It's been a while since I've felt so exposed." I murmured shyly.

"What do you mean it's been a while?"

"Nothing. It's a long story, and…"

Lightning lit up the sky followed by another loud crack of thunder. I gripped his hoodie tighter before he spoke. "I think we have all the time in the world right now, so speak your mind. Tell me."

"I'm too tired to tell you right now." I lied. "Plus, I'm still not comfortable to tell you all that yet."

"Funny you say that with your face buried in my chest. But… I'm here whenever you're ready. I'm pretty sure I'm not going anywhere."

"I hope not."

"Oh, weren't you the one that said you could do this by yourself? Miss tough lady."

"Yes… but I find it much better with company. And even better with company like you." I flirted. I don't even know why I said that out loud honestly.

"Oh yea? And why is that?"

"You're really going to milk this aren't you?"

"Oh, you already know I am. So…? What makes me better company?"

I sighed. "You just are Maureese. Ok." I was trying to cover up for my out loud thoughts. "Now go to sleep."

He rolled me over gently and hovered slightly above me. "Oh no. Tell me!"

I laughed as he tickled me. "No."

"Tell me!" he repeated.

"Ok. Ok." I finally broke. My sides hurt from laughing.

He raised up off me and laid back down, pulling me close to him once again. "That's what I thought."

"Well, for one, you're very nice, and very helpful. Like... you don't let me do everything by myself. You look out for me. So far from what I can tell you have my back."

"I do have your back. I told you that from the jump." he interrupted.

"You have my back." I said, changing my words without hesitation. "Umm..." I paused then giggled to myself a bit before continuing. "You're very handsome." I blushed a bit and buried my face in the front of his hoodie once again. "And so far, you are easy to get along with. You seem like you care." I took a deep breath as a faint sound of thunder cracked in the sky. "So, what do you think about me?"

"The same." he simply said.

I lifted my head up and I heard him smile as I poked him. "That's it? Really?" I laid my head back down on his chest and listened to him breathe. "That's messed up."

He hugged me tight. "Well, even though you were hard to get along with in the beginning, you seem pretty cool. I like how you have your opinions and how you listen to mine. I think we work well together. Plus... you're amazingly beautiful too."

I felt myself blush again as I buried my face and listened outside. "I think the thunder went away. Thank goodness. I love the sound of the rain though..."

"It's so peaceful right?"

"Yesss!!! And it smells great too."

"Good cuddling weather." he added.

"Did you have a girlfriend before all this happened?"

"Nah. Some crazy nut chick I was talking to that claimed me, but no. She wasn't my girl. I was about to cut her off soon anyway. She was a lunatic."

I laughed softly. "Why was she a lunatic?"

"I was telling her I didn't want a relationship with her because she was fuckin around with all these other dudes when I was trying to be serious with her. So, I started to fall back and what not. So, when I did that, she decided to want to make something serious, and I told her it was too late. She didn't like that and started lying on me and calling me all kinds of names. Said I was cheating on her... I'm like, how is it cheating when we're not together? She keyed my car, tore up my house, tore up my possessions... It was bad..."

I laid there in shock as I listened to his story. "How long were y'all talking?"

"A few months. Maybe like six."

"And all this happened in six months?"

"Yea. It was like, I couldn't get rid of this bitch. She would show up at my job, hawk me down, wouldn't let me talk to anyone, and I mean ANYONE. Not my friends, not my family, no one without her asking who it was..."

"Did you comply with her? Like, when she asked you who it was did you tell her?"

"At first. Before I figured out what she was really about. But after a while, that shit got old, and I stopped. She was a straight hoe, and I didn't know until she fucked one of my boys. He showed me a video of her sucking his dick and everything."

"Oh wow!!" I blurted.

"Yea. That's when I fell back, and that's when she started hawking me and what not."

"Well damn. What the hell did you do to that girl?"

He laughed hard. "What did I do to HER? Nothing. She was just an overly jealous bitch. Guilty conscience I guess."

"I meant... You must have put it down on her to make her get that way. She didn't want anyone to get her good goods." I teased.

He laughed. "Got you. Nah, mean, I do my thing though. Put it down nice and slow, rub you down, make you feel good. Find all the right spots." My lady parts tingled a bit as I could imagine his hands on me. He went on talking. "Play with it a little bit, make it nice and wet before I slowly slide in."

"Oh, my gah! Ok!" He was turning me on with just his words and he had to be stopped before I attacked him.

He laughed again. "What? You good?"

"Oh hush, you know what you were doing. Don't even act like you don't."

"I was only telling you a story." He was still laughing. "So, what about you? Were you talking to or dealing with anyone before this? Have a boyfriend possibly?"

"Well, nothing like your crazy ass story, but yea. I had a little boy toy I called over every now and then. Not often though. We were talking for a while, but somewhere down the line, shit went sour, and he didn't want anything serious anymore, but I was addicted to the dick, and he was addicted to this good good here, so we kept it as is. He called when he needed some, I called when I needed some."

"When was the last time you saw him?"

"Or do you mean to ask when was the last time we fucked?" He smirked. "Yea."

"It's been a few months. I fell back. Like, at first, it was cool, but then I realized I wanted more. So... Yea. It's been a little while. What about you? When's the last time you had some?"

"About two weeks."

"That's it? Lucky ass."

"Nah. Not even. It was terrible and a quickie with that crazy chick. I just did it cause I needed a nut bad. I hate quickies. I like to take my time with it. Let her get hers before I get mine and..."

"Ok. Ok." I interrupted again. "I get the picture. Gah damn!"

I felt him laughing under me. "I'm sorry Luv. I didn't mean to get you hot and bothered."

"I definitely think you did." I said sarcastically.

"That was never my intention."

I yawned as my eyes grew heavy. My body ached. I fidgeted around anxiously. "What's wrong?" he asked.

"I can't get comfortable. My body aches and my feet hurt. Everything just hurts." I complained. I slid off him as he sat up and turned the lamp on dimly. "What are you doing?" I whispered angrily. My eyes now hurt from the unexpected light from the darkness.

"Hush." he said, and sat at the opposite end of the tent where he began to massage my feet. "Feel better?"

It took me a minute to respond, but finally, I uttered, "Yes. Oh mah gah yes!" I laid back down on the cot. "Thank you so much."

"No problem."

After a little while, he switched to my other foot and his strong, firm hands on my feet felt amazing. It relaxed my whole body, and I laid there paralyzed for a moment. He turned the light back off and laid back down next to me. "You don't want one?"

"Nah. I'm good."

"You don't want anything in return."

He paused. "One thing about me, I do things because I want you to be relaxed, or comfortable, or whatever the circumstance, not because I want something back in return." He snapped a little bit.

"I'm sorry." I snuggled in up under him again for warmth.

"No need to be sorry. I just thought you needed to know."

I yawned. "Ok."

"You think you can sleep now?"

"I think I can manage." I closed my eyes and focused on the peaceful rain fall that had returned outside of the tent. The horrid images still flashed in my mind just as the lightning kissed the skies above us. I tried to shake them away, but they remained. I stayed awake for some time before drifting asleep, falling deeper into the nightmares that awaited my arrival.

As Ready As Ever

The ground trembling under us woke us up and the both of us held on to each other tight until it passed. Neither one of us moved for a while, but unfortunately, I had to go to the bathroom, causing me to leave his side and find a tree.

After realizing I had forgotten tissue, I called out to him, but he didn't respond. It wasn't until I whistled our whistle that he popped his head out and asked what I needed.

"Can you bring me the wipes?"

He disappeared and reappeared behind me handing me the wipes over my shoulder. I laughed at him.

"What's so funny?"

"You not trying to stare at my naked ass."

"It's kind of hard, so I'm gonna leave you be."

After getting myself situated, I made my way back into the tent. "Aww you made us breakfast? Thank you."

"Yea, something like that. And you're welcome. Feel better now?"

"Much."

After we ate, he went to do the same as I did earlier. Oh I wish I could trade places with a guy just for the sake of having to tinkle. Well, take a piss as he would call it.

I finished up my pears and threw the can outside. "What the fuck?!" he yelled from outside then came back in covered in my pear juice.

Laughter erupted from me as he sat down next to me and gave me a look. "You think this shit is funny?" His voice was stern, and I stopped laughing.

"Yea, you're covered in pear juice. I didn't…"

"You think this shit is funny?"

"I'm sorry. I didn't mean to." I stared him in the eyes as I spoke trying to read him.

He moved closer to me, and I leaned back a bit not sure of what his next move was going to be. "I'm a joke to you huh?" he yelled and hugged me smearing the juice all on me.

He began to laugh as he laid me down and tickled my sides which caused me to laugh as well.

"Still think this shit is funny?"

"No."

"I can't hear you."

"No Maureese, it's not. I'm sorry. I'm sorry."

"Didn't think so."

The rest of the juice was wiped off his face before he changed into a new hoodie. As he was taking the wet one off, his shirt came up a bit allowing me to see a little bit of the chocolate goodness that lay beneath it. I couldn't help but to look. He didn't see me. At least, I didn't think he did.

Cautiously, I moved around in the tent to grab myself another clean hoodie as well. He looked at me weird. "What's wrong with you?"

"What do you mean what's wrong with me?"

"You're acting funny. What's wrong?"

"You kind of scared me." I responded shyly. I looked him in the eyes then turned away again.

"I scared you? How did I scare you?"

"I thought you were really mad. I didn't know what you were going to do. You seemed so serious, I couldn't tell if you were joking or not."

"What, you thought I was going to hurt you?" I didn't say anything after his statement, only looked at him with submissive eyes. He turned towards me in a more serious manner. "I would never hurt you." He grabbed my hands sternly. "You hear me? NEVER. Don't even think that way. Not even if you piss me off will I lay my hands on you."

"Ok." I simply said.

"You ready to pack up and move out?"

"And go where?"

"Find something we can really hunker down in. Something more secure than this."

I sighed. "I guess so."

He tapped my leg and began to get out. "Get everything together in here. I'll start outside."

Everything on the inside was folded, packed up and the bags were tossed out one by one. When he finished outside, he came to help me take everything out while I put my socks and boots on. The material from the tent was removed and folded before the skeleton was taken down. Everything was going smoothly until it was time to pack the tent up in its bag.

"No, it goes this way!" I insisted.

"How do you know? That doesn't even look right. Plus, that's not how I remember taking it out." he argued back.

"Ugh… Just try it! You never know!"

"It's not right, why would I try it?"

"Maureese!! Stop being stubborn and just try it."

We were both beginning to get frustrated with each other. I just walked away for a moment and let him do it. Over and over he tried to shove the tent in the wrong way until he finally tried to do it my way and it went right in. I wanted to yell, "I told you so." But I decided not to. Just was happy that it was all done.

He threw the tent bag over his shoulders after putting the camping bags on first. Of course he left me with the lighter ones that I either threw over my shoulders or held in my hand. "If you need me to carry something, let me know. I don't want you to drain yourself."

"Will do Sweetheart." We both looked around as we started

walking trying to figure out which direction to go in. "I have no idea where to go." His eyes glanced at me who was trailing along behind him as he stopped.

"I don't know either. Somewhere by water?" I took the lead walking, and he followed. "Do you know where any rivers or streams are around this area?"

"No, not at all."

"I guess we'll keep walking until we find one." I said trekking deeper and deeper into the woods, or so we thought. In reality, we had no sense of direction and it seemed as though we were walking in circles at times.

"Oh, by the way, you were right about the part." he said, out of nowhere.

"About the what?" I was confused.

"The tent part. About how we needed to turn for it to fit. You were right. I should have listened."

"Well thanks for acknowledging that. I know it takes a lot for a man to say when he was wrong."

"What?" he said,. I just looked at him with innocent eyes and a smile, and he let it go. "So, what did you do before all of this happened?"

"I worked a shitty job and hated the people I was staying with. What about you?" I kept it short. Not wanting to go into too much detail about my troubled past.

"Where did you work?"

"Doesn't really matter now does it?" I exclaimed.

"It matters to me. I would like to know." His voice remained calm.

Me on the other hand, was beginning to get upset. "No. It really doesn't matter anymore. It's probably all gone. Thank Goodness. On to the next bullshit."

I felt him looking at me, but I didn't bother to look back at him. "You have so much anger built up inside."

"Tell me about it." I mumbled.

"It's not good to hold on to it or have it all bottled up. You see what it's doing to you?"

"So what. I'm supposed to talk to you like a psychiatrist?"

"I'm not saying that at all. Just stop being so damn hot headed with me. I'm only trying to get to know you better, but you make that shit impossible. I can tell you're such a caring person, but no one wants to deal with a shitty attitude." he barked, and stormed ahead of me, leaving me to contemplate his words.

Once again, tears streamed down my face as I followed slowly behind him. I hated thinking about my past, and everything they had done to me. He would never understand what I had to sustain. What I had to go through to make it this far. And he would never understand if I never opened up and talked to him about it. In due time I guess. I'm sure everyone, even he, had skeletons in the closet. I'm just not sure if their skeletons are quite as bad and numerous as mine.

He finally turned back and looked at me. I knew my eyes were red and puffy. They still were watery, and I didn't even attempt to wipe them dry. A blank stare was on my face as the thoughts and memories engulfed my mind. I felt numb. Didn't feel real at the moment. I was so lost in my thoughts I didn't notice him walk up beside me.

"Natalie!" I finally heard him say.

I looked at him finally coming out of my trance. "What?" I uttered.

"What's wrong? You need a break? We can stop for a sec."

I cleared my throat. "I'm fine, we can keep going."

"You sure? You don't look too good."

"I said I'm fine!" I snapped.

He didn't say anything to me, just walked by my side. "I didn't mean to make you upset. It's just that... you are so difficult to communicate with at times."

"I know. I'm sorry." I simply said. My statement was stale.

He stopped and stopped me as well before taking the bags off of my shoulders, then off of his. My face was wiped dry, and he sat me down for a little while. He dug in the bags and handed me a bottle of water that he practically had to force me to drink.

"I used to be a personal trainer. I enjoy helping people get fit. I loved going to the gym and weightlifting. I was in the middle of packing. About to move into a new place in the next month. I was so excited to finally be able to leave my parent's house. Be out on my own again. Ya know." He looked down and then took a sip of his own water.

"I feel you." I said. "My parents died a long time ago." I paused. "A car crash. I was sent to stay with my uncle and his daughter. They treated me like shit. Just wanted the money they were getting for taking care of me but for the most part, I took care of myself."

I only brushed over the top of the circumstance only because I could tell he really wanted to know. That he truly cared. "I used to work in a liquor store. Honestly, it wasn't that bad. It was just long hours. But I was happier to be there than to be at home. If that was what you wanted to call it."

I stood to my feet and dusted the dirt and mud off of my pants. "Come on guy, let's keep moving". My bags were swung over my shoulders once again as I watched Maureese do the same. I felt a little better telling him a little about myself, but still wasn't completely sure if he was ready for the long, sad story of Natalie.

Hours were spent walking and we didn't even know where we were going. Little to no destination in mind. My entire body ached as we trekked aimlessly through the woods. The ground trembling under our feet never seemed to go away, but it did seem further than before. Good.

Maureese dropped his bags to the ground and turned to me. He looked just as exhausted, if not more, than I did. "I think we can stop here for the night. It seems quiet enough."

"It's not even dark yet. I think we should keep going. We still have about an hour of daylight."

"It's going to take about an hour to set this shit up. Plus, I'm beat for the day."

"You're right." My bags dropped to my feet as well before I rubbed my shoulders in pain.

The both of us started setting up the tent for the night. Once the structure was complete, he went to put the stakes in the ground while I made the cot for us to lay on. We both threw our bags inside and rested for a while. Same routine as yesterday.

As I sat there, I let out a long sigh thinking about what was to become of society. Were there any other impacted areas? Was there anywhere safe to go? What was the main cause of all of this? While I sat with my thoughts, he was looking for something for us to eat. A can was held up for me to see and I nodded my head. Soon, it was opened and handed to me, and I slowly ate it. I really didn't want it, but knew I had to eat something.

I felt his eyes on me, but I didn't bother to look back until he spoke. "What's wrong?"

"Just thinking is all."

"About?"

"What's going to happen? Will we have to live like this forever? When is it all going to end and go back to normal?"

He looked down, then back up at me again. "You can't think like that. Think about the now. We are here now and surviving."

"But for how long? How long will we just be 'surviving'?"

"Try not to think about it right now. It's been a long day. And we will survive for as long as we have to. Until this all blows over."

I turned the lamp off and laid back next to him and listened to the still air outside of the tent. There weren't even crickets chirping as we laid there in the silence for a while. I shifted about uncomfortably trying to find a suitable position to lay in.

"What are you doing?"

"I can't get comfortable. I'm sorry."

He pulled me into him, and I laid my head on his chest while his strong arms wrapped around me like a security blanket. His breath breezed past my face as I listened to the steady beating of his heart. It seemed to help settle my nerves.

How Far

I rolled over and found myself alone in the tent. I sprang up and looked around as my heart began beating faster in my chest like it had done so, so many times these past seventy-two hours. My palms grew moist from the anxiety that was slowly creeping up on me and I sat still for a while, thinking. Listening. Waiting for leaves to rustle under familiar, heavy footsteps. But nothing came. I had to use the bathroom but was too afraid to move. My stomach growled. I ignored it. I just listened to the still air around the tent, waiting to hear signs of life. Nothing.

Hours passed me by until I finally had to go to the bathroom. As I did, I looked around nervously. There weren't any traces of Maureese. Hunger took over and I nibbled on a can of pineapples and waited inside. Finally, off in the distance, I heard the rustling of leaves and heavy footsteps. I flipped open the tent flap and peered out and I could see him walking towards camp with things in his hands. Relieved, I sprang out and ran to him, jumping on him making him drop everything he held.

"What's wrong?"

"Nothing, I was just worried about you. I woke up and you weren't there. Where did you go? What took you so long? What happened?" I bombarded him with questions.

"My bad. I was gonna wake you up, but you were knocked the fuck out. I didn't want to wake you up." He looked down. "Where are your shoes?" He scooped me up in his strong arms and brought me back to the tent before going to grab what he was holding in his hands and came back.

"I thought I'd go and see what was around. I found a few stores and got a few things is all."

"What did you get? How far was the store?"

"About an hour's walk. All that walking we did yesterday, and it seemed like we went nowhere. Walked in damn circles. I just got more food and water. I also found something else." A large grin appeared on his face.

"Something like what?"

"You have to come with me to see it."

Without hesitation, I began putting on my boots. "How far is it?"

"It's not that far. I need help packing this stuff up first."

"It can't wait? I want to see what you found."

"You will, no worries. Just, help me pack up first."

I rolled my eyes and sucked my teeth. "Fine."

In no time, we had everything packed and out of the tent and the tent was taken down and packed away. Correctly this time. It seemed like the take down was much faster than yesterday. Either we were getting better at it, or the anticipation got the best of us.

As we started to walk, I glanced over at him who was looking at me with a big smile on his face. It made me smile a bit.

"What?"

"So you missed me huh?"

"Maybe just a teeny tiny bit. Maybe. What's it to ya?"

"Nothing. I thought it was cute."

My loose strands were brushed behind my ear as I tried to cover up my blushing face.

A half hour passed and a small cabin with brown shutters that was overrun by nature came into view. After seeing it, I picked up the pace and he followed after me.

"This is what you found?" I asked and peered into the hazy window, but it was merely impossible to see through it.

"Yea. This is what I found. I think we could most definitely hunker down here for a while."

"Is it safe?"

"I don't see why it wouldn't be. I didn't go inside yet. I don't think anyone has been in here for years."

"Why do you think that?"

He pointed at the bottom of the door. "If someone was coming in and out, the leaves would have been moved."

Our bags were set down by our feet before he grabbed onto the old doorknob, turned it and pulled the squeaky door open. Nothing but stale air came out as the both of us cautiously peered inside and shined the light around to get a better view.

"Wait here, I'll go check it out."

I was about to argue with him as usual, but stopped knowing there was no changing this man's stubborn mind. So, outside, I waited and looked around to ensure no one was nearby. From a different perspective, I probably looked suspicious, like we were robbing the place or something. I laughed to myself at this thought until I felt a touch on my shoulder and jumped back.

"It's clear. Let's bring our bags in."

"What took you so long?" I whispered.

"There's a basement. I checked that out too. I don't think you have to whisper Nat. We're the only ones around."

He walked around me to grab a few of the bags and whatever bags were left were grabbed by me and brought into the grungy space. The door closed behind me, and I looked around the studio cabin.

The windows were disgustingly dirty right along with the floor that had dirt, grime and build up on it. More lights shined through the cracks between the windows and the wood of the building than through the windows themselves. I sighed as I put my things down. I guess it was better than living in a tent right?

"This place needs a lot of work man." he said,, scratching his head and looking around.

"You think it's an alright place to stay in for the long term?"

"I actually think it is. Welcome home."

"Some home." I uttered and walked further into the space. "What to do first?"

"Clean this bad boy up."

"What's downstairs?"

"I'll show you. Come on."

The narrow staircase led to a dark and dank room below the main cabin. The room was a large open space with a dirt floor and brick and mortar walls. Only a few items cluttered in the corner. A few pieces of furniture and an old run-down sink that had stains that told their own stories.

I covered my nose for the smell was much worse than it was upstairs. "What is that smell? It smells like something died in here."

"Something did die in here."

My eyes cut over to him as I began to walk back towards the stairs. "What?"

He laughed and grabbed my arm gently. "I'm just kidding."

I hit his shoulder. "That shit is not funny, Maureese."

"I don't know what the smell is but I'm glad it's not upstairs."

My light danced around the dark room until it stopped on something on the other side. "I think there's another way out. Does it open?"

There was another set of steps that he walked over to and up that led to a set of Marcello doors. He unlocked it and was about to open it.

"Wait!" I yelled. "Don't open it. Something could be on the outside. At least we know it opens."

The door closed and locked again before he came back to my side and examined the hot water heater I was standing next to.

"I wonder if this thing works."

47

"It looks pretty beat up, but wouldn't it be so nice if we could take a hot shower?" I closed my eyes and could feel the hot water on my skin already. Feel the cleanliness a hot shower would give me.

"That would be nice." I had a feeling he was envisioning the same thing I was.

"Can we get out of here now? It gives me the creeps down here."

Once we were upstairs, my eyes scanned the main cabin again. "Where do we start in this place? I'm not sitting down in here, let alone laying down."

"We have to get a few cleaning supplies then. You ready?"

I shrugged my shoulders. "I guess so."

A few emergency bags were packed with a few survival items. Flashlights. Water. Some cans of food. I handed him one before we walked out of the cabin. Before we walked away, he examined the doorknob.

"We need to get something to lock this with."

"I'm sure we can find something. Which way are we going though?" I looked around the endless forest waiting for his response.

He grabbed my hand and began to lead the way. "About a half hour walk this way."

Hope for the Better

Just as he said,, a half hour walk later, another shopping plaza came into view. Cars were crashed and everywhere on the road along with scattered body parts. Some cars had bodies in them, while others were just abandoned, or blood stained.

From the woods, he looked around for a while ensuring it was safe to go down. My head was hung low gathering the willpower to go down into the chaos. Finally, he made the move and drug me down the shallow hill to the parking lot. We stayed low and close to the abandoned cars and tried to avoid stepping on the shattered glass that was everywhere on the asphalt. It was merely impossible to do so.

"Shit, this sun got me baking. I should have left this at the house." he said,, removing his hoodie.

I stopped mid stride and stared into an empty car that was splattered with blood. Windows broken out. The smell of death burned my nostrils once again before I was tugged along by Maureese. His bare arm wrapped around my shoulder as we kept moving.

As usual, he went into the grocery store first to scope it out. I leaned up against the wall keeping a lookout for any movement out in the distance. I was soon distracted at how eerily quiet it was. Minus the flies buzzing around in the cemetery. No cars sped by. No planes flew over-head. Not even the bright and welcoming chirps of birds. Sweat dripped down my forehead and I swiped it off taking a deep breath.

My mind wandered as it usually did. I was glad that I wasn't living the life I had before all of this but was kind of upset and worried at how things turned out. Thoughts of "What is to come next?" "What now?" and "Who else is out there." flooded my mind once again until my thoughts were interrupted.

"All clear."

"Do you think we're the only survivors?" I asked walking to his side.

"We can't think about that right now. We have to get this shit done."

"Anything good in here?"

"Some fresh fruit and vegetables that I already grabbed up. Some canned food, cereal… regular pantry stuff."

"I guess I'll go this way then. Anything in particular you want?"

"Anything but beans. I'm tired of those shits." He tried to joke to change my mood, but I was already down. My thoughts were slowly taking over and winning.

A fake smirk spread across my face before I walked down one of the aisles where I browsed for a bit until I found something worth grabbing and stuffed them down in my bags. More canned fruit. More canned vegetables. Some canned soup, tuna fish and juice.

I swung the half full bag back over my back and it almost brought me down as it dropped. Ignoring the weight, I kept moving through the aisles. Some noodles we couldn't cook. Cereal with no milk. A few containers of peanut butter I grabbed, and a few bags of bread to go along with it.

In the next aisle, I met up with Maureese who was grabbing cleaning supplies off the shelf. I joined him before he stopped and turned to me. "How you feeling?"

Little to no emotion was on my face as I looked up at him. "I'm doing ok. Just trying not to think of anything, but it's hard."

He grabbed my hand briefly with his free hand and brought it up to his face. His soft lips kissed the back of my hand instantly sending chills throughout my body before he continued what he was doing.

I glanced down in his bag and saw paper towels, cleaning rags, bleach, window cleaner, paper plates, plastic cups, eating utensils, trash bags, and a few rolls of toilet paper.

"You think that place has running water? We should have checked before we left." I asked suddenly.

"I don't even know. I damn sure hope so. I could go for a shower right now. My balls are hot and sweaty."

I looked at him with the stank face and a smile spread across my face. A real smile this time. "That is too much information."

"I'm just speaking facts right now." he said,, smiling back. Noticing my change in attitude, he added, "Welcome back."

"I'm going to take this to the front and get another one. This one is almost full."

At the front, another smile ran across my face as I shoved a few things down in my bag and made my way back to him.

"I found some candy bars and chips. What kind do you like?"

"I don't really eat that stuff. It's bad for you. Do they have any peanuts?"

"You want some more salty nuts?" I smirked.

He paused for a minute and burst out laughing. "Yea, I'll take some more salty nuts."

Back where the candy was, there were some peanuts that I grabbed up and he met me where I was standing. "I think that's all for now. There are still a few more stores we gotta hit up. This shit is getting heavy."

"Should we make another trip then?" I questioned following him to the front.

"Yea, but I think we can grab a few more things before we head back. Tryna get as much as we need to hold us down for a minute." He took the lead once more as we headed out the door towards a pharmacy.

"Want me to go in first?"

"I think we're alright."

I grabbed the door handle and proceeded in cautiously looking for any signs of movement, but he brushed my shoulder as he took back the lead back. I stood in one spot while he scouted the place anyway.

"We're good." he yelled from the back. I walked about the aisles grabbing pain killers, toothbrushes and toothpaste, and feminine products. Just as I grabbed the tampon box he came around the corner. Of course. He didn't say a word, just walked past me as if he didn't see what was in my hands. I laughed to myself and continued to empty out the boxes in my bag to save room.

Whatever else I thought was necessary was grabbed up as I kept strolling down the aisles. Deodorants, chap sticks, soap, washcloths and a few towels etc. The basic need items.

I ended up at the front where he was standing there waiting for me. "You ready?" he asked, picking up all his full bags.

"I'm ready." I grabbed the remaining bags. Although he left me the lighter ones, they were still pretty damn heavy.

"Try not to think of it and walk fast." It was as if he was reading my mind. As if he knew that I was complaining to myself about this damn walk.

We headed out the door, and across the hot, stinking parking lot, and disappeared into the thick of the trees. Not much was said on our way back. There was just heavy breathing and haste.

The leaves crackled under our boots. The sound echoed off the bark of the trees. The wind whistled through the treetops and swept down and kissed the sweat that was accumulating on my forehead and the rest of my body. The sun was playing hide and seek in the clouds, and when it shone upon us, it showed no mercy on our backs.

As soon as we entered the cabin, our things were thrown carelessly to the floor. I wanted to lay down so bad, but there wasn't anywhere to do so. Instead, I found myself sitting on the dusty floor as I tried to catch my breath. Fresh, squashed fruit was handed to me before he sat down beside me.

He rubbed his shoulders as he ate his over ripe banana. I looked at my aching hands as I ate mine. His eyes danced over me, and I could feel his gaze until I met his eyes with mine and he smiled. "What?" I asked in a soft, sensuous tone.

He shook his head. "Nothing. Nothing at all." He rested his head back on the wall. "I'm so beat. I need a nap so bad."

"Yea, well good luck with that. Where are you going to lay?" I retorted.

He thought for a minute as he ate before he stood up and walked into the kitchen and turned the faucet on. After a much-anticipated wait, the water ran down into the sink. Excitement was on his face as he turned to me who was already on my way over.

"What the hell! I can't believe it works!"

"I know right." He turned the hot water on, and we waited. Only cold water continued to run out. "Wishful thinking huh?"

"Just a little bit, but I'll take the cold water for now.

The water was splashed on my sticky, dirty face giving me instant satisfaction and relief. He left my side and began digging through the bags searching for who knows what.

"What are you looking for?"

"A rag, I'm about to wash my ass quick fast."

"In the kitchen sink?"

The wooden floor creaked under my boots as I made my way to the bathroom and flipped the light on by instinct. I was actually surprised when the light didn't come on. Water came out of the sink and bathtub and even the toilet flushed to my amazement.

By the time I walked out into the main cabin area, he was already undressing. I quickly turned around and covered my eyes. "What are you doing?"

"You thought I was playing? I'm about to really wash my ass quick fast. I can't take this nasty feeling no more." I could still hear the fabric coming off of his body. "Like you've never seen a naked man before."

"Ok, but that is not the point." I laughed. "Go in the bathroom, the water works in there too."

"Too late." The water came on, and I could hear the rag get in the way of the water hitting the sink bottom.

I just stood there, with my back towards him, not knowing what to do. Still in shock that he was really bold enough to 'wash his ass' right in front of me. No remorse about it either.

"Can you hand me some soap sweetheart?"

"...sure." I responded back and handed him a bar once I found and opened it.

It was so hard for me to resist the urge to not look at his naked and perfect, muscular physique and even harder to not reach out and touch. It was like his body was calling out to me to do so. I bit my lip and walked away to the bags and pretended to look for something to distract my mind from the sexual thoughts that were swirling in it.

His heavy footsteps walked towards me before he reached into the bag nearby for clean clothes. As he did so, I shifted about nervously and he laughed.

"Why are you acting so shy?" he asked.

"I don't want to be rude and stare."

He laughed again. "You. Not be rude?"

"You know what the hell I mean Maureese."

"I'm dressed now, relax." he said,, still behind me.

I lowered my hands away from my face and looked over at him only to discover he was only wearing sweatpants. No shirt. I turned away quickly but oh how I didn't want to. His body was so fine. So, toned. "I thought you said you were dressed." I said with bass in my voice.

"I am. I'm decent." he paused again. "Oh, come on. This is too much skin for you too?"

"Yes."

"Oh gees, fine." He came back and hovered dangerously close to me and grabbed a shirt to put on. I was convinced he knew what he was doing to me. "Better?"

I looked back at him as he put the shirt on and was able to catch a small glimpse of his impeccable physique before it disappeared under his clothing. "Much. Thank you." I relaxed and came back to my senses as I dug in the bags, looking for something this time. Clothes and a rag for myself that I took with me, along with a light into the bathroom.

"Ahhhhh!!!" I shrieked. He came running to my side.

"What?" he yelled looking to find what was yelling for.

I pointed to a big ass bug that was crawling up the wall.

He laughed at me again. "Really?"

"I wasn't expecting it to be there! I'm not scared." I reached up to grab it, and the motha fucka jumped. I jumped back, threw my hands down and walked out the bathroom. Maureese was in tears at this point.

"I got it for you. Go ahead and do what you gotta do." he said, walking out of the bathroom still laughing.

"It's so not funny Maureese. Not at all." I said in a joking manner before closing the door. An uncomfortable feeling came over me, so I opened it back up slightly and began to undress.

The cold water ran over my rag before I hit all my hot spots and lady parts with it. I rinsed the rag and wiped my body down several times to get all the dirt, sweat and blood off. Feeling somewhat refreshed, I put my clothes on, gathered everything up and headed to the main room. A smile appeared on my face as I looked at what he was doing while I was washing up.

"I need you to work your magic like before." he said, smiling back at me.

My clothes were tossed to the floor before I grabbed the blankets he handed to me and took them into the tent that was now set up in the middle of the floor. The blankets were laid down how they were the previous night and I stepped out to admire our work.

"I'm so glad you did this. I'm too tired to even clean this place up right now."

"Yea, I thought you might like it." He stepped back and held his hand out. "Ladies first."

Without hesitation, I went in and laid down on the semi-soft cot and relaxed. He laid down beside me and we both stared at the top of the tent in deep thought.

I rolled over and looked at him. "What are you thinking about?"

He moved closer and invited me into his arms. My head rested comfortably on his chest as his arms wrapped around my waist. "Nothing really. Just satisfied with today. That nothing bad happened and that we are alright." He played in my tangled hair as usual.

I paused. "Do you feel that?"

"Yea, I feel it. I just can't wait for it to stop."

"At least it seems to be going away."

But the rumbling never seemed to cease. All day, we could feel it come and go. Some appeared closer than others, but they were there nonetheless reminding us of the damages and lives that were and have been destroyed by the creatures. It happened so often now, sometimes, I couldn't even notice them. But then, there were times like this, where we could still feel them.

"Damn it!" Maureese blurted out of nowhere.

"What?"

"I forgot to grab a lock."

"We should be alright for the night. We're in the middle of the woods."

"Yea, and WE still found this place. Other people like us may find it too. What do you think would happen?"

I pondered for a minute. "I don't know. I can only hope for the better but fear the worse. You feel like going back out to get one?"

"Hell no. Not today at least. Sit up for a minute." he requested, and I abided.

Outside the tent, I could hear him move the bags in front of the door before he came back to lay by my side. His body heat warmed me as he brought me in closer to him.

The wind blew hard against the cabin and eventually came in through the cracks in the wood. The covers were pulled up to my neck as he fidgeted around to adjust to the new cover placement. When he did, the covers between us moved, and I could feel the heat pour off him.

"Why are you so hot? I'm freezing over here."

He looked over at me. "I'm always hot. ALWAYS."

"You're like, my personal heater." I laughed.

"I'm seriously about to start sweating though. These covers are killing me."

"So, take them off. No need to be uncomfortable."

"I'm about to." he said, but didn't move for quite some time. I could tell he was deep in thought about something.

"What's on your mind?"

"Just thinking about my family. My brother especially. I miss him so much man." His voice got weary the more he spoke. "I miss his laugh and how silly and awkward he was." He sniffled and then got up and left me in the tent by myself.

As he got closer to the bathroom, the light got dimmer until it disappeared altogether when he closed the door. His silent sobbing and the wind was the only sound in the cabin.

I laid my head back and tears streamed down my face as well. Not because something upsetting was on my mind, but simply at the fact that he was hurting. He always portrayed to be bad and hard, like nothing really bothered him. I'm just glad he was able to let out his bottled-up emotions.

The sun was almost gone as I laid there and listened to the wind sweep the raindrops onto the cabin's exterior. Sleep slowly began to take over me when I was rejoined by Maureese. His back was turned, and no words were spoken. I rubbed his back before turning and pressing mine against his and falling asleep.

Chemistry

A loud crack of thunder woke me from my deep slumber. Maureese's arm was tightly wrapped around me, but he was still asleep. I don't know how. The cabin was still dark as I laid there for a while watching the lightning flicker through the windows. The sound of the rain against the house was so peaceful and calming now that we weren't out in that mess.

My body ached from the hard and laborious work it had endured these past couple of days. Not accustomed to lifting, toting and running as much as it had been doing lately. I rubbed my shoulder gently before running my fingers through my tangled, knotted up and dirty tresses. Something seriously needed to be done about its current situation.

Maureese shifted behind me, and I rubbed his brawlic, bare arm soothingly. "Why are you up?" he muffled.

"I can't sleep is all. Go back to sleep."

He shifted to lay on his back as he stretched. "What are you thinking about?" he whispered, completely ignoring my request for his continued rest.

"Why do you think I'm thinking about something?"

"You're always thinking about something. So what's up?"

"Go back to sleep Reese."

I heard him smile. "I like that. Reese. No one really called me that before."

"Really? That's like, the first thing I thought of."

"I told you, my friends and family called me Mar since I could remember. The name stuck with me."

"I feel you. I'll be right back." I began to crawl over him to leave the tent, but he stopped me while I was hovering over his body. His action startled me, as I found myself in this very awkward, yet pleasant position.

"Where are you going?"

"I have to pee if that's alright with you."

He chuckled. "That's fine. My bad. Here." His grasp loosened before he handed me a flashlight.

"Thanks."

My boots were slipped on my feet as I proceeded to the bathroom. When I crawled over him to get back on my side this time, he didn't grab me, but I was kind of hoping he did for some reason.

"My turn." he said,, leaving my side with the light. I watched as it slowly disappeared into the bathroom.

The lightning and thunder finally subsided as I lay there on my back as sexual and intimate thoughts ran through my head. I brushed them aside when he returned and once he settled down, he invited me to lay on his chest. I did happily before he embraced me and began to play in my hair.

"How old are you?" I asked abruptly breaking the silence.

"Twenty-nine. Just turning. What about you?"

"Twenty-seven. Should be turning twenty-eight one of these days."

"When's your birthday?"

"October thirty-first."

"Halloween? Really?"

"Yea. You gonna talk the Halloween bullshit to me?"

"What do you mean?"

"People always call me devil child or devil worshiper cuz of my birthday."

"Seriously? That's childish."

"Tell me about it. So, when is your birthday?"

"August tenth. Had a party and all. Drinks, girls, weed."

"Wait... you smoke weed?" I interrupted.

"I used to. Why do you sound so surprised?"

"I don't know, you just don't seem like the weed smoking kind of person."

"Yea, I smoke here and there. Would kill for a blunt or some liquor right about now." He paused. "You smoke or drink?"

"I used to. I could go for a drink right now my damn self." I giggled a little bit. "I still don't see you as a smoker though."

"Welp, I am ma'am."

My mind back tracked to the times that I used to drink and smoke. Good times when I used to hang out with my friends. My REAL friends. Not those fake tramps that pretended to be cool with me only to talk shit behind my back.

"Damn, I can't sleep now." he said, randomly interrupting the silence. I felt him sit up from underneath me. Then he moved and left the tent.

"Where are you going?" I whispered. He didn't answer me.

The room lit up with the light of the lamp and he poked his head in the tent. "Why are you whispering? We're the only ones in here."

I shrugged my shoulders and repeated louder. "What are you doing though?"

"About to start this damn cleaning process."

"Really? Now? In the middle of the night?"

"Why not? You have somewhere to be in the morning?" he contested.

"No... but Reese, the light. Is it too bright?"

The light went off before he cuddled up next to me. "I don't know what to do with myself!" he gruffed.

"I told you to go back to sleep." I laughed.

"Had to make sure you were alright."

"Yea, sure, blame it on me. I told you I was fine. You don't listen."

He didn't reply to my remarks as we laid there quietly. At first, my hand was simply on his chest, but after some time, he held it gently in his and locked his fingers in mine while rubbing them. This simple gesture allowed the chemistry between us to grow wildly. It was strong and a bit frightening to me at the same time which caused me to pull my hand away and rest it back in its original position.

"Are you ok?"

"I'm fine. I'm going to try to get some sleep. I'm planning on getting this place cleaned up." I lied. Truth is, his soft, yet manly touch was turning me on, and I was afraid of this strong feeling that was growing for him.

"Sure." he simply said. I felt his arm fall limp to his side. I think he knew I was lying. "Goodnight."

"Goodnight." I closed my eyes and tried to force the sleep and finally, it came.

There's A First for Everything

Slowly, my eyes opened to scuffling around in the kitchen and I peeped my head out to find Maureese cleaning up a bit. Before heading over to him, I stretched and watched as he wiped the front of the cabinets down with a rag.

"How long have you been up?" I grabbed a rag and joined him.

"I never went back to sleep. Just waited for the sun to come up and got to work. Go check out the bathroom."

The rag in my hand was placed down as I hastily made my way to the bathroom. The sink was wiped out and was as clean as it was going to get along with the tub and the toilet. After using the bathroom, I went back out to where he was.

"It looks amazing. I feel like I can sit on the toilet now." I complimented picking my rag back up to work.

He opened the cabinet doors. "I cleaned these out as well. Want to start putting the food away while I finish?"

"I can do that."

"What happened last night?" he asked as I began to put the food away.

I turned around and looked at him, who was now looking at me. "What do you mean?"

"I thought we had something going. We were… connecting and you stopped."

I looked away and continued my task. "I don't know what you're talking about."

"Yes, you do Nat, what happened?"

I looked back at him but could hardly keep eye contact. "I don't know. It's just…" I stammered over my words as I tried to get my thoughts together but decided to keep it real. "I barely know you, and it felt kinda… weird."

"Weird? Weird how?"

I slowed down what I was doing and faced him. "Like… I don't usually fall for people and especially not that fast. It took me by surprise that I felt that connection with you so soon, you know." I took a deep breath.

He continued wiping down the doors. "I'm sorry. Didn't mean to make you feel like that. I'm in the same boat, it's just something about you I like. A lot. We have a different type of connection. A different kind of understanding I guess."

"You don't have to apologize. I understand what you mean." I picked up the pace with my work just as he did. "I just don't open up to people like that. All of this is new to me. It freaks me out a little bit, especially because I feel this connection with you, and we literally just met. I don't know how to deal with it."

"I'm not mad or anything, just wanted to know is all."

I nodded and grabbed the now empty bag and brought it back to its original spot. I dug around in the other bags trying to find some with food in it. Instead, I felt a large metal object and pulled it out but dropped it immediately and he turned to me.

"What's wrong?"

My eyes glanced over at him. "When did you get the gun?"

"I grabbed them up when we were at the camping store."

"What the hell Reese. Why did you grab it?"

"All this shit going on. You really thought I wasn't gonna grab a few guns to protect us with?"

"What do you mean a few? There's more?!" I took a few more steps back.

"There's like four more down in there… Why are you stepping back for?" he interrupted himself.

"I've never seen one of them up close before. Is it loaded?"

"It's not loaded but the bullets are in there too."

"Why didn't you tell me you got them?"

"I was, just didn't get a chance to yet." He walked up to me and held the gun out by the barrel for me to take. "Here."

"I don't want that." I took another step back.

"Take it." he demanded.

I didn't move. "I don't even know how to shoot it."

He came to my side calmly. "This is the clip where the bullets go. This is the trigger that you pull to shoot. This is the safety." he said, pointing, then he flipped the switch. "On. Off. Make sure the safety is off when you go to shoot."

"I'm not going to shoot."

"If it comes down to life or death, you better shoot. Just make sure the safety is off." He held it out again for me to take it. "Here. It's not loaded."

Finally, I took it into my hands. "Maureese, I can't..."

"Don't ever say you can't. You want to survive right?"

"Yea, but..." I stammered.

"Then you survive and learn. You don't know what or who we will come across, so it's better to be ready for whatever comes. "You understand?" His voice was stern.

"Yes, it's just... I never shot a gun before. I've never even held one before."

"No worries, I'll teach you. There's a first for everything."

He walked away from me to continue what he was doing in the kitchen area as I examined the weapon in my hand more closely.

"I'll show you how to load it in a minute. We can find you one that you're comfortable with, but you're gonna learn how to shoot them all."

"How do you know so much about them?"

"I used to go to the gun range a lot with my friends." he said, without looking at me.

"Have you ever… Shot something or… someone before?"

He turned around and looked at me while he rinsed out the rag in his hand. "No. And I hope I never have to." He turned back around, and I walked over to him and placed the gun gently on the counter.

"Ok."

"I'm sorry. I should have told you sooner."

"It's cool." I went over and grabbed more bags searching for more with food. Once I found them, the contents were put away in the cabinets.

"You still trust me?"

"Why wouldn't I? Is there anything else you grabbed up that I should know about?"

"Some pain meds. That's about it."

As he worked on the last cabinet, I buried my face in the back of his hoodie and wrapped my arms around his waist before pulling away to continue putting items away in their respective places.

When the food was done, I moved on to the medicine. He wasn't lying when he said, he got pain medications. Some of what he grabbed were heavy hitting like Vicodin and Percocets along with some antibiotics I hope we would never have to use. Nonetheless, they were filed away in the bathroom medicine cabinet along with some over the counter pain medicine. After that was done, I moved on to the toiletries until most of the bags were completely empty.

"Nat." he yelled from the main room. I went to see what he wanted. "I'm about to load these up. I want to show you how to do it."

I hesitated before walking over to him as he was pulling out all of the guns and bullets that were in the bag and laid them out neatly on the counter. He had so much patience with me as he walked me through the steps of loading the bullets into the magazine and telling me the basic knowledge of guns. The different types there were. Warning me about the recoil.

I watched adamantly as he loaded the bullets one by one into the clip. The process looked so easy until it was my turn to load them, and I found out... It wasn't as simple as he made it look. It was hard at first and eventually caused the tips of my fingers to hurt, but I didn't let the pain deter me from doing what needed to be done.

The clip was loaded into the gun. "That's it?"

"That's it. Just make sure it clicks when you put it in there, cock it back and you're ready to go." He handed me the gun by the barrel, and I took it firmly.

"It's loaded?"

"Yea. The safety is on though. Remember, before you shoot..."

"Take the safety off."

"And if you take it out, you better be ready to shoot. Don't flash it around and act all tough with it. You pull it out with intent to use it."

My eyes danced over the gun. "This shit is sexy." I blurted, now a little more comfortable with it.

He laughed. "You like that one?"

"Yea, I like it. Still have no idea how to shoot it, but it's nice as hell."

"Here. Load this one up and I'll load these up." Another gun was slid over to me, and the bullets were placed in between us as we worked.

A few minutes later, I finished loading the clip and moved on to the next one. "Check you out. A little while ago, you didn't want to have anything to do with them."

"I think I've been educated enough to understand. But loading magazines and shooting are two completely different things."

"I got you. I'll teach you how to use it. But for now, we need to go get a few more things."

"Like what?"

"The lock for one, and something to fill those gaps to block the wind from coming in. But I don't know what to get to do that." He scratched his head.

"I think I know what to get. Do you know where a hardware store is?"

"Yea. I know where one is. When do you want to go?"

"Whenever you're ready I guess. We can finish cleaning when we get back."

"Let's go now while it's still early in the day." I began to get ready to leave and so did he.

"Did you eat today?"

"I can eat later. I'm not all that hungry at the moment."

"You sure you don't want a squished orange?"

I shook my head and took the orange he held in his hands as he put his gun holster on. I really wasn't all that hungry, but knew he wasn't going to let up until I ate something. No matter how small it was.

After gearing up and grabbing our extra bags, we set out through the woods to our regular shopping plaza. As we walked along, our arms kept bumping into each other. Shyly, I intertwined mine around his as we winded through the trees, and thick brush. He held on to it tightly.

As we approached the plaza, a small hardware shop came into view. As I went to take a step in, he pulled my hoodie back which caused me to stop. I looked at him like he was crazy.

"What are you doing? I go in first." he whispered.

"Why do you always go in first?"

"Cuz I…" he paused and exhaled hard and put his head down. "I don't want you to be…" he paused again. "Just let me go first."

I looked at him precariously before stepping back and letting him take the lead. A short moment later, he whistled for me to come inside.

"So, what do we need to get now?" he questioned once I was close.

Slowly, I scanned the aisles until I found what we came for. Several cans of expanding foam were grabbed and I handed them all to him to put them in his bag.

"That should do it!"

"What is this stuff?"

"You basically spray the foam in there and let it expand to fill up the gaps."

I looked at some of the beautiful displays that were in the store. Some fancy bougie shit that I could never have afforded in my previous life. I kept moving until we reached the door.

"The locks!" He turned around to look for some while I waited at the front for his return.

It took him a while, but he came back with a new door handle set and a few tools. He shoved them in my bag before grabbing my hand, leading the way to the camping store. And once again, I waited outside while he scoped the place out until he called to let me know it was clear.

"Why did you have to scope this place out? We were here just yesterday."

"A lot of things can happen in one day."

"What do we need from here?"

"Whatever you think we will need Nat."

More shirts, hoodies and sweatpants were shoved carelessly in my bag before I moved on to the socks. A few packs of them were grabbed for Reese and me. As I was putting them away, he came up beside me and looked at what I was doing. I showed him the pack I grabbed for him. "Are these your size?"

He started laughing. "Those aren't going to fit me. I have big ass feet."

I raised my eyebrow and looked down. "I see."

"These are more my size." he said,, grabbing another pack off the shelf along with a few packs of boxer briefs.

I sighed. "Lucky you. I've been commando for the past few days. It feels weird."

"Why not get boxers?"

"They're uncomfortable. Especially under sweatpants. Not for me. I miss my underwear." I whined.

He moved closer to me. So close, I could feel his breath on my spot on my neck as he whispered, "What kind?"

I moved away and shoved his shoulder. "Perv." I laughed ignoring the sexual chill that he gave me. I came close to him. Closer than he had gotten to me and whispered. "Purple lace booty shorts." I stepped back and looked at him with flirty eyes and a devious grin.

He looked at me surprised then smiled. "That must be a sight to see."

I wandered down the aisles and gathered whatever else I thought would be handy. Another pair of boots, a small radio, a walkie talkie set and a few pocket knives and fire starters. By the time I was done, he was by the gun counter, and I headed over to him.

One by one, guns were packed into his bag along with more and more bullets. Above the counter, there were large rifles and shotguns that he grabbed up too and put in a new bag. As we were walking, something caught his eye and he stopped and smiled as he reached up and grabbed it.

"What is it?"

"A propane heater. We won't be cold tonight!"

As I read the box, small tanks of propane were grabbed off the shelves and placed by his side before a few were put into an extra bag.

"How long do you think those little ones will last?"

"At least for the night. We'll have to come back and get the larger ones."

"You ready to head out then? We already have so much stuff to carry back." I whined.

"I'm ready. Let's go."

All of our bags were put on our backs or carried in our hands as we made our way back to the cabin we called home. The heater box I carried wasn't heavy, but it was awkward as hell, and he looked like he was struggling a little with the heavy bags he had in his hands, but he didn't complain. Just kept moving like I did.

Speechless

The walk back felt longer than usual and with each passing minute, each step we took, the clouds got darker, and the wind picked up more. The smell of rain was strong until...

"I felt a drop Nat, we gotta pick up the pace."

"How much further is it?"

"Another ten minutes."

It began to pour down and we both found ourselves struggling to sprint back to the house with all the items and extra weight in our hands and on our backs. The only thing that helped me keep moving was the thought of not getting all of this stuff wet and have it not work.

He reached the cabin before I did and disappeared into it before returning to take a few things out of my hands which helped me run a little faster. Everything was thrown on to the floor as the door closed behind me and I paced around to help catch my breath.

Not only was my hoodie soaked, my shirt and pants were too, which only made me shiver as the wind blew in through the cracks in the walls. I shoveled through my clothes to find something to wear and made my way to the bathroom, stripping off my wet clothing on the way. I felt his eyes on me as I did so. Admiring me. I couldn't help but to blush as I cracked the bathroom door and took my painfully cold shower.

When I reached for my towel, it wasn't there. In my haste, I forgot to grab one. "Reese!" I yelled out. There wasn't a response, but it seemed as though he knew exactly what I needed for only a short minutes later, a towel was thrusted into the doorway.

"Thank you!" I said as I quickly dried myself off. But even doing that didn't relieve my body from the shivering. The shirt I put over my head hung off me like a dress because it was his. The sweatpants I grabbed turned out to be a hoodie, but I threw it on and shook my head at my carelessness.

My clothes were hung up in the bathroom before I headed out to the main cabin where I was met by a soft gaze. I froze as I looked at him and my eyes began to wander down his bare chest to his impeccable abs. My eyes lowered and I bit my lip as whole sexual fantasies flashed in my mind.

He smirked and pointed over to a small orange light that glowed brightly before he stood up and walked over to me, pushing me closer to the heater.

"Stand here and get warm. I'm going to take my shower."

His voice was unusually deep and very tantalizing as he spoke and looked me up and down like he was having the same fanatic visions I was having. Butterflies flew in my stomach as he breezed past me and disappeared into the bathroom. Damn. That man had a strong hold on me.

Sweat began to accumulate on my forehead and my palms grew moist as I stepped away from the heater. It was no longer needed. He heated me up with just his words. The thoughts were shaken from my mind as I put on a pair of sweatpants for the night. His yells from the cold water hitting his skin echoed throughout the cabin and I couldn't help but to laugh just as he had laughed at me.

Our things were everywhere and so unorganized and I hated not being able to find what I wanted when I looked for it. But that would have to be dealt with later. Right now, my main concern was trying to seal the holes in the walls so the heat would stay inside, and the cold and rain would stay out.

The spray foam was applied to one side of the wall and expanded and filled the gaps just like it was supposed to do. I stepped back to admire my work just as he was coming into the main cabin area. He ran right into me. I'm not entirely sure it was an accident though.

"My fault." he said, as he helped me catch my balance and proceed over to our clothes.

I couldn't take my eyes off him that was in nothing but a towel that was tightly wrapped around his waist. Water still dripping off. Chocolate skin glistening in the low light. I stood there speechless. My mouth opened, but no words came out as my eyes danced over his protruding muscles that were inviting me to touch.

The urge was too great not to and I found myself slowly approaching him. My hand reached out and answered the invite and made contact with his chest. Slowly, it moved down to his abs, and he stood there watching me touch and admire him with no complaints or no actions to stop me from doing so.

My hand pulled away when I came to my senses and walked into the kitchen area to compose myself. The urge to want to do more than just touch was strong as I took a few deep breaths to calm them. What the fuck was he doing to me? Why was I feeling this way towards this man? Why was he so God damn sexy?

Just as I had somewhat relaxed, his warm embrace came from behind me and held me tightly to him. Thank goodness he was now fully clothed.

"What's for dinner?"

"What…" My voice was soft, and I was still distracted by my thoughts. I cleared my throat. "What do you want to eat?"

"Heh…" he smirked. I had a feeling he was thinking something other than food. His voice was still deep and sexy. "Umm…" he cleared his throat as well. "What kind of soup do we have?"

I opened the cabinet and rattled off a few choices. "Chicken noodle, beef, potato and bacon…"

"I'll take that one." He interrupted and reached up past me and slowly grabbed the can. I think he knew what he was doing to me and enjoyed watching my reactions.

His can was opened and placed on top of the heater to warm up as I made my decision for what I was going to eat for the night. My can was also placed on the heater to get warm before I joined him in the tent sitting a good distance away from him.

"We need a few chairs in here."

"I saw some earlier, but we had all this shit in our hands." he replied.

"We got a lot of stuff today didn't we?"

"Indeed we did and yet it seems like we didn't get enough and still need more." He got quiet and looked around. "I don't hear the wind as loudly anymore and it feels warmer."

"I sealed one of the walls with the expanding foam." I said getting up and checking the temperature of my can. It was to my satisfaction, so I grabbed it off the stove and began to eat.

"There's no way that is warm yet."

"I don't like hot food. It's perfect to me."

He stood up and examined the completed wall. "It definitely made a big difference."

"I will finish when I get done eating."

He checked his can and took it off. I guess impatience got the best of him and he chugged his food down completely before I could even get halfway through mine.

When I was done, I took the can into the kitchen and began to rinse it out. His heavy footsteps came up behind me and soon, I felt his body press up against mine pinning me between him and the sink. His lips came close to my skin before he gently kissed the back of my neck which caused me to flinch and lean forward. But that didn't stop him. He followed me down and kissed the back of my neck again ever so softly.

I lost my breath, and my mind went right along with it before it came back and I pushed him away, turned around and looked at him with low eyes. His eyes were low as well as he bit his lip. Waiting patiently for my reaction. I couldn't keep my eyes on him for too long and turned away, but he wouldn't let me look away for too long. My chin was held in his hand, and he used it to lift my head up so that I could look at him again. Every time I tried to look away, he would place his face in my view until I relented and looked him in the eyes.

He began to pull my chin towards his face, but I unwantedly pulled away. He smirked. "Can you wash mine too please?"

He was so nonchalant about it, like nothing just happened between us just now. I had forgotten what I was doing. Too caught up and mesmerized by him and the feeling he had given me.

"What?" I stupidly asked.

He moved in close to me and spoke again in a deep, sexy voice that only made me lose my train of thought again. "Can you rinse the can out for me please?"

My eyes closed as I nodded my head and he pulled away from me, disappearing in the tent. I lavished in his scent that still lingered around me for a while before turning and hovering over the sink asking myself, 'what the fuck just happened?' A few deep breaths were taken to regulate my racing heart before I began to rinse the cans out. They were thrown in the trach before I joined him in the tent a good distance away.

For some reason, I couldn't look his way even though I could feel his burning gaze on me from time to time. Maybe it was because of this feeling he gave me? But whatever the reason may be, the urge to want to be with this man only intensified.

"You ready?"

"Ready for what?"

"To finish the walls. I want to see how you did it."

I had completely forgotten about it, but I stood up and we both went over to an undone wall with expanding foam in our hands. I showed him how simple the process was, and he continued to fill the gaps on that wall while I worked on another until we met in the middle. Gaps completely filled. The both of us admired the work and soon, the temperature in the room grew too hot causing us to turn the heater off.

"I'm gonna go through all these bags. I can't stand not being able to find what I need when I need it." He said, emptying out a few.

I giggled to myself a bit. "I was thinking that earlier."

All of the things were sorted and filed away, and we were losing natural light fast. The clouds only made it disappear faster.

"Should we turn off the lights Nat?"

"I think we should. We can finish cleaning up tomorrow. I'm getting tired anyway."

"We need curtains for these windows, so we don't have to worry about being seen."

I sighed and looked around. "There's so much shit we need to do to make this place decent to live in."

"Good thing we have all the time in the world." The back of my neck was kissed again, and I flinched. He found a new spot. A strong one at that. One that I never knew existed before he came along and discovered it. He knew what he was doing to me, and no one made me feel quite the way he made me feel. Actually, no one had even come close.

Side by side, we laid in the tent on our backs. Usually, I would have my head resting on his chest, but tonight, I kept my hands to myself not knowing what trouble they may bring my way.

My hand was gently grabbed and kissed. "Are you alright?"

"I'm fine." I lied. Truth is, I wanted him, and I wanted him bad. I was all hot and bothered and wanted him to satisfy this desire but at the same time, I didn't. Not yet anyway. He was still a stranger.

"You sure?"

"Yes. I'm sure. I'm fine. What else do you think we'll need to get tomorrow?" My words were only used as a distraction.

"Curtains and chairs for one."

"I need some personal care items. Like my African black soap, a brush, shampoo and conditioner…" I rattled off feeling the cleanliness of my hair in my head. "And a razor!"

"Those aren't necessities."

"They are to me. I really want to exfoliate, but the water is too damn cold to do that."

"What's exfoliate?"

"Where you scrub your skin. Get rid of all the dirt and dead skin cells. This soap and washcloth just ain't hitting the spot. Even if I had my African Black soap, that would make me feel so much better." I could still smell the fragrance my favorite soap gave off. The way it made my skin feel. Squeaky clean. Something so simple that I took advantage of when I had access to it.

"I miss my Mirage soap." he said,, nodding in remembrance too. "Not the blue one. That shit stinks. But the green one... The green one was my shit."

I burst out laughing. "They smell like shit though?"

"Yeah. I can't stand the other ones."

"Well alright then."

"What else, what else? More food I would suppose." he said,.

"We need to get more propane." I interrupted. "Those are high priority." I paused briefly. "We need a cart or something, so we don't have to keep carrying this shit all around on our backs."

Our conversation was interrupted by the trembling ground off in the distance. I rolled over and put my head on his chest and allowed him to hold and comfort me until the trembling went away. Even after it did, I didn't move and grabbed his shirt and held it tight. He didn't say a word and allowed me to do so as he gently rubbed my back.

We never got back to our original conversation although it was still on my mind of everything else we needed to get tomorrow. Under me, his breathing grew steady and his grip around me loosened as he left me alone with my thoughts. I tried to force myself to sleep and after a long while, it finally came.

The Grueling Task

The sky slowly lit up through the trees as I picked out a fresh apple and hoped it was still good. I took a big bite and as I chewed, my lips smacked from the enjoyment of the sweet, juicy fruit.

"You smack any harder Imma get hard." His groggy voice startled me for it literally came out of nowhere.

I stopped chewing and giggled. "What?"

"What the hell are you eating? It must be good."

"I'm eating an apple, and it really is good. You want one?"

"Not right now. I'll get one later. How long you been up?"

"Not too long." I took another bite, chewed and swallowed before I spoke again. "How long you been up? I'm sorry if I woke you."

"You good. Been up for a few minutes. Enough to hear you smacking on that damn apple." he laughed. "Why are you up though?"

"I couldn't go back to sleep."

"Again? Something on your mind?"

"No. Not this time. I had to go to the bathroom and was just… up afterwards."

He emerged from the tent and headed to the bathroom but on his way, he stopped and gave me an unexpected good morning hug. In no time, he was back by my side asking if I was ready to get the day over with.

"Do we really have to? We can't just relax for the day?"

"We have mad shit to do. We can rest when we get it done. Go and get dressed. Let's go while the day is still young."

I rolled my eyes, grabbed some outside clothes and got changed in the bathroom. By the time I came out, he was already changed and packing up the emergency bags. I joined him before gearing up for the trip. A few hunting knives attached to my pants. My boots laced up tight.

The truth is, I really did just want to lounge around all day cuddled up next to him. Let our bodies rest up a bit but he was right. I hated that he was right, but we had to get shit done.

We trekked through the woods until we came up to our familiar plaza. The first place we went was to the food store and filled up an entire camping bag with food. On our way to the next store, we grabbed a few carts and cautiously rolled them out, stopping every now and then to ensure we weren't attracting any unwanted company. When we were sure nothing was coming and were relieved that the ground wasn't shaking uncontrollably underneath us, we proceeded to the pharmacy.

The carts were left at the front while we ransacked the place grabbing up any and everything we thought we may need or that may be useful. Some of the things I grabbed were more toiletries, first aid supplies and cleaning supplies. I was also able to find my favorite shampoo and conditioner along with combs, brushes and other items that I could use to help tame this knotted up stuff on my head that was desperately calling for help.

There were a few other things that I grabbed in hopes to help get rid of the stale smell that seemed to be permanent in the cabin. A few fragrant sprays, incense and scented candles.

In the stationary aisle, I grabbed some notebooks, pens and pencils. I made my way into the feminine aisle and grabbed more feminine products for myself and soon, found myself staring at condoms. I began to walk away but came back to them. I walked away again and came back. I couldn't believe I was thinking about sex at a time like this, but that didn't stop me from shoving a few boxes of them in my bag. I heard his heavy footsteps coming and moved a little further down the aisle and tried to play it cool. Hoping he didn't notice the big empty space on the shelf.

"You ok?" he asked quietly.

I pushed loose strands of hair behind my ear and replied nervously, "Yea, I'm fine." I could hardly look him in the eyes yet again. "How are you? Are you ok?"

He looked at me puzzled. "Yea, I'm good." He turned away from me, then looked back. "Are you sure you're alright?"

I looked up at him. "Reese, I'm fine."

"Ok." he reluctantly said and went on about his business.

I let out a soft sigh of relief and went into another aisle and my eyes lit up at what I saw. Female underwear! Finally! They weren't the cutest things ever, but it sure as hell beat the shit out of being commando. I wanted to throw them on right then and there but didn't want to be tasked with having to unlace and lace up my boots.

As I was grabbing a few more toiletries for myself, some things I had seemed to look over, I spotted the Mirage body wash that he was talking about last night. So, I grabbed a nice set for him. The green one like he said, and tucked it securely in my bag along with battery operated clippers.

Blankets and pillows were grabbed and stuffed away in my bag along with some black out curtains that would be useful and threw the full bag over my shoulder before walking to the front.

My bag was placed in one of the carts and I whistled out to Reese who returned my whistle back. It seemed far off in the distance, and we played a short game of Marco Polo until I was at his side in the food department. He had nearly cleared the shelf off.

"What did you get?"

"Anything and everything. I'm sure between the two of us, we'll eat it all." He looked at me and smiled. "You ready?"

"Yes!"

"You get everything you need?"

"For now."

"Well damn, how much stuff do you need?"

I glared at him and nudged his shoulder before I began to walk back to the front. He followed close behind. After we grabbed our carts, we left and headed towards the camping store where he checked it out before he allowed me to come in.

"Propane, chairs… and what else?"

I thought for a moment trying to remember what we had discussed the previous night, but my mind was drawing a blank, so I simply shrugged my shoulders.

"I guess anything else we missed the first time?"

He chuckled and began to leave my side. "In and out."

Slowly, I walked up and down the aisles trying to scope out anything we may have missed. Something caught my eye and made me smile as I pulled the box off the shelf and drug it to the front of the store. My cart was emptied out completely to make room for the box, then repacked like puzzle pieces to ensure that everything would fit properly. Clothing was wrapped around everything, and I hoped that they would hold it all in place so the loose items wouldn't fall out.

After that task was done, I went back for the chairs that looked so comfortable and brought them to the front as well and tried to figure out how they would all fit.

"What are you doing?"

"Rearranging a few things. I found something you are going to like." I said with pure excitement in my voice.

He looked at me puzzled and when I took too long to answer he asked, "What is it?"

A smile rolled over my face as I moved from in front of the cart exposing the box and what was on the cover. "I found an air mattress and a battery powered air pump!"

He moved closer and examined it closely. "Good shit! What size is it?"

"Queen! No more hard floor and tons of blankets."

"Good shit Nat." he repeated. "I came up here to get a cart though. I found bigger propane canisters."

"How much room do you need in the cart?"

"Empty it out. It's quite a few of them plus the little ones on the shelves."

"Should we just get another cart?" I questioned removing the items as he requested.

"Not sure how we would navigate three of them, but if you can figure that out, be my guest." He took the cart and rolled it in the direction he had just come from.

Foolishly, I really sat there and tried to figure out a way that we could push three heavy ass carts through the woods. Impossible. Two would have to do.

By the time I walked up on him, he had already put two-twenty-pound propane canisters into the cart and was working on the third. A fourth one was down at his side. While he worked on that, I started taking the little ones to the front and placing them in between the gaps of what was already in the cart. Clothes were then wrapped around them to hold everything in place. Hopefully.

"We're going to have to come back. There are a few more in the back we have to get as well."

"These won't be enough for the winter?"

He shook his head. "They only last nine hours. We're going to have to get a lot more tanks and conserve the heat if we're going to make it through winter comfortably."

"When do you want to come back then?"

"Today if possible. If not, then tomorrow."

"Are you ready to roll out then?" I tugged on my cart and it slowly began to move. "Are these going to make it through the woods?"

"Only way to find out. Let's go."

The bags that didn't fit on or under the carts were put on our backs or around our arms as we pushed the carts out of the store and across the parking lot. Instead of going through the woods like we usually did, we walked the road until it was time for us to head back to the cabin.

Pushing the carts up the hill was the absolute worst and hardest part about the walk. Over one-hundred pounds in either cart was no joke, but somehow, we worked it out and managed. We made our way through the deep, thick woods leaving cart marks behind us from the weight of them in the dirt and fallen leaves. We tried to cover our tracks as best we could hoping no one would be able to follow them. I'm sure with a good rainfall, they would go undiscovered.

The cabin came into view, and I was filled with joy and relief as it did. This was one hell of a walk, but we did pretty well once again with our findings. One by one, we unloaded each item from the carts and brought them into our humble abode. We pushed the carts away from the cabin and left them in a bush nearby so as to not raise any suspicion.

The new chairs were unfolded before we plopped down in them and rested back trying to catch our breath from our journey and tasks. Neither one of us said anything as we sat there together. Nothing filled the room for a while except heavy breathing and a lot of sighing of relief.

"You think we'll have enough time to go back and get those other tanks?" I finally asked after some time had passed. He said, nothing for a while, just looked at me with tired eyes.

"Do we have the energy is the real question."

I stood to my feet and looked outside to see where the sun's position was in the sky. "The sooner the better right?" I said with very little enthusiasm. I didn't want to go, but I didn't want the feeling of having to go at a later date linger over my head either.

He came over to where I was standing and looked outside at the sky as I did. "Let's get it over with."

"You ready?" He held out his hand for me to take and I took it.

"As ready as I'll ever be."

We walked back outside and to where we had left the carts hidden, grabbed them and made our way back to the familiar plaza. Before we got too far, I stopped, and he stopped with me.

"What's wrong?"

"We forgot our supplies bag."

He turned and looked back at the house. "I'll grab the supplies bag. Any more bags we need, we'll grab while we're out. I'm not emptying out any of them right now. Just want to get this done and over with."

He came back rather quickly, and we continued walking to our destination. It always seemed like it took us no time to get there but took forever to get back. When everything was normal, it was always the other way around.

We reached the camping store and went in directly to the back where the propane tanks were. One by one we loaded most of them into both of our carts. Seven in total. Of course, I was given the cart with less weight in it.

"You ready?" he asked me, but he already knew the answer. He already knew I was dreading this trip back home. I simply did a tired nod, and began our walk.

I thought the last time I pulled this cart was heavy? That didn't even compare to the weight I was pulling and pushing now. Even getting through the parking lot was a task. Maureese assisted me the best he could by pushing his cart into mine. It helped some, but I know it was hell on his body.

The same route was taken as the one before. Shadow the woods on the street before it was time to head back up through the tree line. Attempts were made to push and pull the carts up the hill, but it was no use. Eventually, we had to take all the canisters out, take them up the hill before bringing the carts up and replacing them in there.

The task was exhausting, and we were both drained of energy, but the journey wasn't over yet. We still had to bring everything back to the cabin.

The sunlight played hide and seek through the colorful leaves of the trees as we walked. They were already changing from bright green to bright colors of orange, red and yellow. Looking around at nature was the only thing that kept my focus off of the grueling task we were doing.

The cabin finally came into view and relief came over me as we got closer to it. It felt like we had been walking for hours tugging and lugging and pulling these heavy ass carts behind us, all a while trying to cover up our tracks at the same time. But it was done and out of the way and hopefully, they would be enough to last us through the winter. I didn't want to have to do this shit again. At least not for a long ass time.

The bags on top of the carts were placed inside the cabin doors when we got there along with the small canisters.

"Where are we going to store these? Are they safe to store in the house?" I asked as we caught our breath.

"What if we put them in the basement? They'll be out of our way, easily accessible and safe from outside."

"Go unlock the basement doors while I bring these over." I had so little energy but knew this needed to be done before we rested so I pushed through.

"How about you go unlock the doors and I'll unload everything. I know you're tired and I don't want you to strain yourself."

I looked at him and shook my head. "I'm not going in that basement by myself." I began to take off a canister and he grabbed it from me before I could put it on the ground.

"Go open the doors Nat. I got this." he demanded.

I rolled my eyes and said, "Fine." before taking a quick stroll to the cabin and over to where the stairs to the basement was. I stood there with my flashlight in my hand trying to pump myself up to go down and open the doors for him.

I took a deep breath and took my first step on the stairs. It creaked. I took another deep breath and began to run down the stairs. Cobwebs got caught on my face and in my hair as I bolted towards the Marcello doors on the opposite side of the dark, dank room.

I fumbled around with the door for a while trying to find the lock to unlock the doors. I began to panic which made me drop the light. It felt like something was closing in on me. I panicked even more. My breathing increased as I could feel the presence growing closer and closer to me. I began to scream and bang on the doors, but they wouldn't open.

Just in Case

Finally, I felt the lock and twisted it. The doors were opened from the outside and the sunlight came pouring in as I raced up the steps, right into his arms.

"What's wrong?" he yelled, holding me tight. He pulled away from me and looked at my face with concern before he wiped the cobwebs free.

"Something's down there!" I yelled. "Something's down there." I repeated.

He looked past me and down into the dark hole. "I'll be right back."

Just as he went to leave, I grabbed his arm to stop him. "No! Don't go down there, don't leave me!"

He cupped his hands around my face and got close. "Nat, I'll be right back. I have to go see what's down there." Tears streamed down my face as he left my side and as I impatiently waited for his return.

Down in the basement from the darkness, I could see his light flashing around searching for what I was so sure was there.

"Nat." he said, in a calming voice when he came back up. I was still a bit hysterical and still crying. "Nat!" he repeated, and I finally focused on him. "Nothing is down there."

I shook my head. "No. I know something is down there. I felt it."

"Nat. Nothing is down there. Look." He grabbed my hand and began to gently pull me towards the door.

I pulled away and screamed. "I'm not going down there!" I began to cry again from fear.

"Nothing is down there. Come on. Have a look for yourself. I'm right here with you. Nothing is going to happen to you, I promise." He took my hand again and aided me down the stairs where he shined the flashlight in our walking path.

At first, I was hesitant to follow his lead, but his strong hold made me feel secure. When we reached the bottom of the steps, he shined the light around the entire room as I looked around confused. Nothing was down there at all. I let his hand go and wandered around on my own, searching for what was never there.

"But I…" I began to speak. "But it… was…" my voice trailed off as I was trying to figure out what the presence was that had haunted me only a few moments ago.

"There's nothing here Luv. Nothing at all. I don't know what you saw. I think you're done for the day." he said, gently guiding me back up the steps and into the cabin where he sat me down.

Confusion was spread all on my face as he handed me some water and a piece of fruit.

"Drink this and eat this. I'm going to go put this shit in the basement. I'll be right back ok. Relax." He disappeared out the door.

I sat there in the silence alone and still very stunned. What the fuck was I tripping about? What was it that had frightened me? I took a sip of the water and a bite of fruit as I sat and contemplated on what the fuck was going on. Was I losing my mind? Or was I tired, drained and hallucinating?

Thirty minutes had passed, and I still sat in the same position he left me in. Water still in my hand and one bite out of the fruit missing.

"How are you feeling?" his voice bellowed through the cabin and broke the silence startling me. I hadn't even noticed him come in the door, close it behind him and walk up beside me.

"I'm feeling better, I guess. I don't know what…" I tried to explain to him, but I couldn't.

"It's ok. Finish your fruit. I'll make you more to eat."

"It's ok Reese, I'm not hungry." I stared blankly at the wall until I focused up on him. "I'm sorry."

"Sorry for what?" He came closer and knelt down beside my chair.

"For having you do all that shit by yourself. I'm sorry."

"Don't worry about it. It's fine." He kissed my forehead before standing to his feet. "Wanna help me unpack all this stuff?" he asked in a cheerful manner.

I nodded my head as I stood to my aching feet. I tried to ignore my sore muscles as we began to unpack the bags and sort everything away in the respective homes. The room grew darker as he hung up the blackout curtains and a light came on soon after. The floors were swept thoroughly and were free from all the debris that clung to them.

My heart raced in my chest as I watched him go over to my bag with the little surprise in it.

"You want me to unpack these too?" he picked up the bag and started to unzip it.

"No!" I blurted out. "I'll get those." He looked at me puzzled before he zipped it back up and gently placed it on the floor. "I want to mop and finish cleaning up so we can relax." I tried to explain. It worked, for his face went back to normal before he began on a new task.

"You still not hungry?"

"No. I just want to get this shit over and done with so we can relax for the rest of the day."

While he filled the mop bucket with water and bleach, I finished sweeping up the little piles of dirt that were left behind on the floor and threw them away. The entire floor was mopped.

I would have helped only, we had grabbed just one mop, so I sat and watched the floors get somewhat clean.

"We're going to have to do another pass at it."

"I'll do it. Go ahead and make you something to eat."

Before I started mopping, he emptied out the bucket and filled it back up for me. Bleach was added, which burned my nose, and I mopped just as he did while he made himself something from the kitchen. The heater was turned on so he could warm his food up. I was glad too because it definitely was getting cold in here as the sun was setting.

As he waited, he watched as I mopped and by the time I was complete, his food was ready and he was eating it. In no time, it was gone. I laughed to myself at the fact of how fast he always ate.

We looked around and examined the work and the progress we had made throughout the day. The place was actually starting to look like a habitable space and the both of us were quite satisfied with the way it was turning out.

"I need to go take a shower now. I feel disgusting."

"Wait, I got you something." he said,, turning me around by my arm before digging around in his bags. A small box was pulled out and it took me a while to realize what it was. Once I did, my face lit up.

"You remembered? Thank you!" I took the black African soap in my hands and smelled it through the box.

"I remember you saying you liked it, so I grabbed it up for you. I hope I got the right one."

"You did! Wait, I got you something too." I pulled out the Mirage gift set along with the clippers and handed it to him. A smile spread across his face as well.

"Thank you." he said,, giving me a big sticky hug.

My clothes were gathered before I made my way into the bathroom where I completed my cold shower routine and got dressed. When I came out with my things, I found Reese patiently waiting to go in with nothing but his sweatpants on. I covered my face and turned away.

"Why, just why?" I asked out loud.

"Why, why, why, do you react like this?"

He walked over to me and moved my hands away from my face and pulled my chin up so I could look at him. I couldn't. Every time I tried to look away, he would move his face to where my eyes wandered to until I met with his eyes. It was only brief before I blushed and looked away.

He smirked, gave me a big hug and went into the bathroom. On the way, I admired him from behind. I couldn't figure out why I couldn't look him in the face at times. Why he made me blush the way he did. I did know that I was beginning to like this guy and the amazing feeling he gave me.

The smell of bleach still lingered around the space, so I decided to light a few candles and incense to try and mask the smell and breathe life back into the house. Once they were lit and had the place smelling a little better, I blew up the mattress after laying a blanket down to protect the bottom in the area I wanted it to lay.

Sheets, blankets and pillows were added to it, and I couldn't wait to nose dive in it. Sleep comfortably for the rest of our nights here. No more hard floors or makeshift bedding. A real mattress would have been much better, but this would do just fine for now.

"What is that smell? It smells amazing." he asked after coming out of the bathroom.

"I lit an incense and some candles to try and get rid of the bleach and stale cabin smell."

Once again, I found myself not being able to look at him as he stood there in nothing but a towel wrapped around his waist. Water dripping down his body. Why did he have to tease me this way?

He was so careless when going through all the bags and when he grabbed his that was nestled under one of mine, it fell over causing some of the contents to fall out. Before I could make it over to where he was, he was already picking things up off the floor and putting it back. I was hoping he didn't take a good look down in the bag before I could get there, but he did. He paused and looked at my bright red, embarrassed face as I stood there frozen from what his reaction might be.

He held up one of the boxes of condoms. "I hope you got a bigger size than these." Well that wasn't the reaction I was expecting. "When did you get these?" he chuckled a little bit, but I didn't say a word as he continued looking through the bag. He pulled out another box and held it up so I could see. "These are the size I need."

I was so embarrassed at the fact that he found them. Ashamed of myself for even getting them. I looked away, then back up at him but his eyes didn't leave me. It was like he was studying me, trying to figure me out, even though I couldn't figure myself out.

"Are you mad?" I asked finally.

Sensing my slight anxiety, he joked. "No, I'm not mad. Just wondering when you're gonna let me use them."

My eyes grew in shock. "I got them as like a... Just in case kinda thing, you know." I stammered.

"I'm not going to rush you." He put the boxes back. "But I'm going to let you know, these," he held up a box, "these aren't fitting me." He smiled and threw it in the bag too before he began to get dressed. I turned away until all of his clothes were on, and he was by my side looking at the bed I put together.

"Is it comfortable?"

"I didn't lay in it yet. I was waiting for you."

He grabbed my hand and the both of us laid down on the mattress and sank in.

It's so much better than the blankets!" I exclaimed as I stretched my entire body over the bed.

He let out a sigh of relief. "Fuck yea it is."

We stayed in that position for about ten minutes before I fully got under the blankets and snuggled in. Another five had passed before he got up and turned everything off, leaving the candles lit and joining me. My head rested on his chest after his invitation to do so and he took my hand in his and played with my fingers until the feeling faded away as I went to sleep.

I Need a Drink

Reese was still asleep when I woke up and the candles still flickered on the kitchen counter. Unfortunately, no matter how hard I tried, I couldn't go back, and I was up and bored. My fingers ran through my hair and so, I finally decided it was time to do something about it.

In the bathroom, I soaked my hair and applied conditioner where it sat for at least a half hour. I shampooed and scrubbed my hair at least three times before detangling it, which took almost forty-five minutes to do. Once it was rinsed and conditioned one last time, I was finally able to style it. Two simple cornrows that ran straight back.

I admired my new self in the mirror and was loving every part of it. With all the tangles, knots and leaves that were in my hair, there was no way to tell that it was actually way down past my shoulders.

Feeling refreshed, I set out to the kitchen and grabbed a can of fruit before sitting down comfortably in the chair as the sun began to rise.

"You up early again?"

I smiled. "I'm up early again. I woke up and couldn't go back to sleep."

"How long you been up?"

"A few hours."

"Something on your mind?"

"What isn't on my mind?" As I rinsed the cans out, his footsteps grew closer, and I braced myself for what was next

"Your hair looks nice." he said, before grabbing me from behind and kissing my neck.

A few deep breaths were taken before I was able to respond back. "Thank you."

He pulled away and turned me around while his eyes danced over me in admiration. "You look beautiful. I mean... you did before but now..." he rambled.

I smirked and blushed. "I know what you mean. Thanks."

He kissed my forehead and tugged on a braid before disappearing into the bathroom allowing me to finish with my initial task. I blew the candle out and looked around as I pondered about what this new day would bring us. What should we do today? What needed to be done?

"What's the plan for the day?" he asked, sitting next to me with his breakfast in his hand. I couldn't help but to giggle to myself. "What's so funny?"

"I literally was just thinking that to myself. I was thinking of having a chill day. Let our bodies rest up a bit. I'm sore." I rubbed my shoulder and watched as he took another big bite out of his food. "Do you even enjoy your meals?"

"Yea, I do. Why?"

"You eat so fast."

He finished in another rather large bite. "No I don't. You just eat slow." The can was rinsed out before he came back to my side where my mouth was still open from his smart-ass comment. His finger closed it for me as he smiled.

Silence fell in the room as we both sat in our chairs in our own worlds. Lost in our own thoughts. My eyes grew heavy and before I knew it, I was slowly drifting off sitting straight up in my chair.

I heard his footsteps stop right in front of me and I opened my eyes to his extended hand. "Go lay down Luv."

I was helped to my feet before being helped into bed and tucked in. A kiss was placed on my forehead before I fully went back to sleep after a bit of tossing and turning. I was so used to him lying beside me or me falling asleep on his chest. When he wasn't near, it was a task to go to sleep naturally, but finally, it came and overtook me.

Bullets clinked together as I sat up and looked to see where the sound was coming from. He was sitting in his chair, loading up the extra clips. I joined him.

"You sleep well?" he asked, not taking his eyes off what was in front of him.

"Yea. How long was I sleep for?"

"A few hours. That's what you get when you stay up all night."

"I couldn't help it. What have you been doing this whole time?" I looked around and something was definitely missing, and a few things had been changed around.

"Nothing really. I put the lock on the door, made some emergency bags in case we need to leave in a hurry. Felt the rumbles until they disappeared. Then got bored and decided to load these clips."

"What did you put in the bags? You need help loading?"

He finally looked at me then back at the clip. I could tell something was wrong. "I can always use your help. And I put clothes, a few extra blankets, food, water, lights, a few guns and bullets and clips down in there. Basic stuff, you know? I put it all in the basement by the doors. I also moved the tent down there." He rambled solemnly. Even though he didn't look up, my eyes never left his handsome face.

"What's wrong Reese?" I finally asked.

He stopped working and hung his head. "My mind keeps wandering. I need a drink."

"Do you know where a liquor store is?"

He turned to me with a blank face. "I do, but it's mad far. Like… an hour and a half walk from here."

"Shit!" I exclaimed.

"Right."

I stood up and peered out a window. "How much daylight do you think we have left?"

He looked at me puzzled as I walked over towards him. "You're not thinking…?"

I nodded my head with a smile. "Yea I'm thinking."

"You're wild." He shook his head and continued loading the clips completely dismissing the thought.

I walked over to him and forced his hands in mine. The bullets clinked together as they fell on the towel in his lap. "Come on. You're not the only one that needs a drink."

"Nat, that's about a three hour walk Hun. I thought today was going to be a chill day."

"It would be a better chill day with some liquor in our systems. Plus, I don't like you like this. Sad and gloomy."

He stared at me with the same blank face then took his hands out of mine and continued to load the clip. My morale felt shattered. I was about to sit down in my chair when I noticed him put the bullets back in the towel and stand up.

"Get dressed." he demanded.

My face beamed. "YES!"

I raced over to our clothes and threw some on. A hoodie, sweat pants, socks and then my boots. Before he could even get his clothes on, I was standing by the door with our bags in our hands patiently waiting for him.

"So, you just gonna watch me get dressed?"

I smiled, "Yup."

He shook his head and smiled just like I did. "You grab any guns?"

"No. I didn't." I began to walk over to where he was.

"Don't worry, I'll grab some… and your knives too."

"Thank ya." I said in a sweet voice.

His two guns were grabbed up along with my knives that I secured to my pants. Before we walked out the house, he handed me an extra key to the new lock, and I tucked it down in my boot.

"You're going to lose that."

"No I'm not. I would have tucked it in my bra but… I'm not wearing one."

His eyes perked up as they glanced down at my chest then back up to my face. He smirked as he interlocked his fingers with mine and led us in a new direction. The sun glistened off the beautiful colors of the leaves giving me a sense of peace that I happily welcomed.

As usual, we shadowed the road from the tree line. Crashed cars were down below, along with decaying bodies and body parts which was our unfortunate reality now.

"We're gonna stop there on our way back." he said, pointing to a gas station.

"Why?"

He cut his eyes over at me. "For propane."

"We need more?"

"I don't see a reason not to get more. I don't think what we have will last the entire winter. I don't know about you, but I'm not trying to freeze."

I nodded my head but didn't say a word as we kept walking. Another half hour away, a new plaza came into view, and we zig zagged through the cars and large gaping holes to the parking lot. Of course, he had to make sure it was clear before he allowed me to walk in but instead of whistling when he was done, he met me by the door.

"Close your eyes."

"What? No!" I snapped back.

He hung his head down. "Please close your eyes."

I closed them as he grabbed my hands. "What's going on?"

"Don't open your eyes."

"Fine." I said and let him lead me blindly. My eyes teared up. "It smells really bad."

"I know sweetheart." he said, still gently pulling me along.

As I walked, I began to slide and held on to his hoodie tightly. "Reese!?" I blurted out frantically.

"Almost done."

We came to a stop and the smell diminished but didn't disappear. "Can I open them now?"

"Yea. You can open them." he replied and let my hand go.

I opened my eyes and found him looking at me. "Bodies?" I asked softly. Sadly.

"Yea."

"How many?"

"Three. Come on." We continued to walk. "What do you drink?"

"Wine."

"Wine? Oh you fancy huh?"

"Ha, no. I like T-Port Wine. You have it before?"

"Nah. I don't drink wine. I like my dark liquor. How does it taste though?"

"It's sweet and tastes like juice, but man oh man does it hit you hard. You would have thought you had some dark liquor."

"I'll try it with you."

"You'll like it. So, what kind of dark liquor you like?"

"Henesy of course. And Morgan Captain Spiced Rum."

"Oh gees. You like that hard liquor."

"It will put hair on your chest."

"Here you go." I said and his laugh allowed me to see his beautiful white teeth. "I'm going this way." I said pointing.

"Go ahead. Just don't head towards the front. And stay alert." he lectured.

"Yes sir." I retorted back.

As I scanned the aisles, I basically grabbed up any and everything I had always wanted to buy or taste but had no money to do so. My wine of course along with some other expensive and reputable drinks. As I walked along stuffing them in the bags, the bottles clinked together.

My breathing slowed and I ducked down in the aisle when I heard shoes scurrying in through the front door. There was a loud crash and the person yelled out in pain. I was guessing he slid in the pool of blood just as I did when we first came in, but he ended up crashing into the shelves in his haste.

My bag was gently placed down by my side and my knife came out of the sheath that was on my hip. It was held firmly in my hand before I got on all fours and crawled to the end of the aisle away from the noise. The guy stood back up again and started walking. I tried to look through the shelves to see where my partner was but couldn't see him. I kept moving quietly.

At the end of the next aisle, I finally saw him knelt down with his gun aiming in the direction all the noise was coming from. I began to move towards him, but he motioned for me to stop and I obeyed. The man's footsteps kept getting closer to where we were hiding and the both of us were ready to go to war if that time came, but we hoped it didn't have to come to that.

The footsteps changed directions before they ended up disappearing completely in the storage room at the back of the store. That was our cue to move. On our way out, I scooped up the bag I had left in the other aisle, tightened it on my back and we both made our way to the front where I froze. He shoved me out the door and away from the bodies he had once tried to shield me from. Clearly, in this new world, there was no shielding from anything anymore. It was what it was.

The both of us ran for another ten minutes until we went into another building and doubled over trying to catch our breath. When I turned around, there were five sets of eyes on us. Two people were holding their guns up at us. Maureese stood up

I NEED A DRINK

strong with his gun pointing at them as well as he pushed me
behind him. Slowly, we backed out of the store. No shots were
fired. It was a simple understanding that we were in the wrong
place at the wrong time, and they let us go.

We ran down the road for a good long while until we came
across the old gas station we saw when we were coming up. The
both of us entered but he held me still at the front while he
looked around. When he disappeared in the back, I got a good
look at what was left in the store. It was a complete mess and
things were thrown everywhere off the shelves.

Over in the mini fridge, there were a few bottles of water
that I grabbed before he came back out with two twenty-pound
propane tanks in his hands. He set them down by the front.

"There are six more back there." He disappeared again.

I looked around trying to find something we could carry the
tanks in. A few wired carts with wheels would have to do. As he
brought forward more tanks, they were placed inside the carts
which only held three.

To fix the noise issue, a few blankets were wrapped around
them to mute the sound. He grabbed two carts, leaving one
behind for me and began to walk out the store. I didn't follow.

"What if the other people need some? Like, the people in
the store."

"I'm not worried about the other people in the store. I'm just
worried about you and me. They're on their own. I'm not trying
to freeze trying to be considerate of others."

"Ok." I uttered in a submissive voice.

My face fell a little as I began to roll the remaining carts.
He stopped me, sucked his teeth and pulled out two tanks from
my cart and left them there before he headed out the door. I
followed his actions this time and rolled my carts with only our
bags in them in either of my hands up to the woods. We
shadowed the road until it was time to make our way deeper into
the tree line back to the cabin.

Shit Can Go Left

The cabin door was unlocked and soon, the basement doors opened where I was waiting. The propane tanks were loaded and stored down in the basement before we made our way back to the front of the house. My boots were removed after everything I held in my hands fell to the floor. The lamps came on and we just looked at each other with pure exhaustion and relief on our faces.

Briskly, he walked up to me and wrapped his arms around me tightly. I stood there stunned for a minute before I held him back. My face was taken into his hands and brought up to his face where he stared at me for a while. Checking to see if I was alright. Quite by my surprise, his lips met with mine briefly before he let me go and walked away.

I didn't move. I stood there startled for a minute touching my lips and reminiscing on his taste. I returned the favor by walking up on him. As he turned around, he was met by my lips. My arms wrapped around his neck while I kissed him slowly. Passionately, before letting him go and walking away. Now, it was he who was stuck and surprised by my actions.

Casually, I leaned up against the kitchen sink and watched him unlace his boots before I went and knelt down in front of him to complete the job. He sat back and relaxed in the chair and watched as I massaged his feet.

"I think I'm ready for that drink now." he said, quietly. His voice was calm.

The newly filled bags were brought over to where we were sitting, and the contents came out. Unfortunately, during the trip, a few of the bottles had cracked and were leaking a bit. The good ones were rinsed off and inspected.

"Please tell me the Henny didn't crack."

"I don't think it did." I replied, handing him the bottle before grabbing mine and sitting down next to him.

The bottom of his bottle was tapped before he opened it and took a big sip from it. Initially, I thought of grabbing a few cups but said 'fuck it' and went bottoms up with my gallon sized wine bottle.

"Check you out. Straight bougie gangsta." he joked.

I laughed and almost spit out my wine. "Nothing bougie over here. You want to try it?" I offered him the bottle and he accepted it.

"I'll give it a taste. You want some?" He offered me his.

No! No! I'm good. Me and dark aren't friends."

"And why not?" he took a gulp of the wine. "Oh shit! This is sweet as hell. You weren't lying about it tasting like juice."

I laughed before answering his question. "I get mad and reckless and want to fight when I drink that stuff. I don't want to have to beat you up in here."

"Oh, so you don't know how to handle your liquor huh?"

"No. I don't know how to handle dark liquor." He took another big gulp of the wine. "Slow down. I don't want to have to clean up anything later on."

"This lightweight shit. It's not going to bother me." He passed the bottle back.

"Yea… it's not as lightweight as you think." I took another small sip. "You might not feel it right away, but that shit sneaks up on your ass."

"We will see."

"So. Do YOU know how to handle your liquor?"

"Yes, I do. I know my limit. I'm about to chill out for a minute. My tolerance is low as hell."

"You feeling it already?"

"I sure do. It feels so lovely right now."

"So how do you get when you drink?"

"Well, I don't get reckless," he teased, "I get more or less chill and laid back. Enjoy the feeling of it. I wish we had some music. I'd dance a bit."

"Let me find out you know how to dance."

"Yea, I do my little two step. Nothing fancy."

"Let me see." I demanded. He stood to his feet and, indeed, did a little two step. We both laughed hard, and drank a bit more.

"I don't think we should go back to where we were today." He got serious.

My face fell a bit. "Me either. Reese, I was so scared. I kind of felt helpless."

"Why is that?"

"I couldn't help you if that guy had seen you."

"You gotta get comfortable with the gun is all. And carry one with you." he said, calmly. "I had it though."

"Yea I know, but still. I should have had your back better."

"Listen," he turned towards me, "I know in my heart that if some shit popped off, you would have done everything you could have to help. Correct?"

I nodded my head and looked down. "Yea. I would have." I looked back up at him. "I think those people lived in that other store. And thank you for leaving them those tanks."

"Yea, I knew you would be upset if I hadn't. But on another note, we know we're not the only ones left."

"That kind of worries me but makes me happy at the same time. Who knows what kind of people we will come across? We got lucky today. What if…" my voice trailed off a bit. "What if next time, we aren't? What if someone comes here? And tries to take this place, or take our stuff? Or someone…"

"Relax Nat. Relax." he interrupted my rising hysteric rant. "We will be ok. If someone comes, we'll take care of it. We will leave. As long as I have you… all this shit doesn't matter at all to me. They are just things. And guess what?"

"What?"

"There will be more things, better things that we can get. I don't want your mind going from hope to loss. Just the other day, you were worried if anyone else was out there. Now we know. Now you're worrying if the people out there are going to come to get us. Rest your mind a bit." He sat back in his chair.

"I'm just trying to be proactive." I said calmly.

"You're going to stress yourself out in the process. We can make plans all we want to but at the end of the day, shit may go left when it was supposed to go right."

He spoke the truth and I sat back in my chair too to absorb his words. Another, rather large sip of my drink was taken before my hoodie came off.

"I so wish we had music. Sometimes, the silence kills me."

He held his drink up. "Cheers to that." He took another drink, and he took his hoodie off too. "What kind of music do you like?"

"Hip hop, R&B, soul. Stuff like that. On my iPod, I had old school, rock, country…"

"Country? Really?" his words slurred a bit.

"Yea, what's wrong with country?"

"You like listening to the banjo and the southern accents?"

"Well, all country songs don't have banjos. They have guitars too." I paused and looked at him but the face he made caused me to burst out laughing.

"You lost points for that one." he joked. "Lost some serious points for that one." He drank more of his drink and stood up uneasily. "Gotta go drain the monster." He slowly stammered to the bathroom.

"Here you go."

I sat in silence, and I knew it would be my turn soon to go. I always had to go every time I drank and once I opened the seal, I'd be going every two minutes. Literally. I took one last sip of my wine.

"I think I'm done. I don't want my head to start spinning." I said randomly when he came back.

"Me too. I hate that feeling." I stood up and began to walk to the kitchen. "Where you going Babe?"

His choice of words caught me off guard, but I just blamed it on the alcohol and brushed it off. "I'm about to go take a quick shower. I feel so sticky and clammy." I grabbed my clothes that were in one of the cabinets and came back to where he was.

"Don't let me hold you up. Go ahead and wash ya ass."

"Reese!" I retorted.

"What? That's what you're about to do right?"

"Yea, but why you say it like that? It sounds so nasty when you say it like that." I began to walk towards the bathroom but stopped as he spoke again.

"Iight. Go and wash your 'lady parts'." he said, mimicking me.

I nudged his shoulder on my way to the bathroom where my cold shower routine was completed. When I came out, he was waiting to go in as well. A kiss was placed on my forehead before he left me alone in the main cabin area with my eyes closed. I absolutely adored his affection.

My teeth were brushed vigorously before an incense was lit along with candles to add a nice calming fragrance to the space. I sat back in my chair and relaxed a bit as I watched the smoke from the incense.

Sexual thoughts ran through my mind once he emerged from the shower in nothing but his towel wrapped around his waist yet again. I tried my hardest to push them away, but today, they were strong. Especially with this handsome man standing right in front of me and this liquor running wild in my system.

108

His tight-fitting shirt and baggy sweatpants were thrown on, but that didn't seem to help any.

"I love that smell." he said, sitting in the chair next to me.

"How was your shower?"

"Fuckin cold, but I feel so refreshed." He leaned closer to me and sniffed. I gave him the side eye and moved away. "Is that you smelling all minty?"

I relaxed. "I brushed my teeth. Something you should do because your breath is rockin right now."

He stood up, but not before blowing his hot breath my way. I made a face at him as he brushed his teeth and smiled to myself. I shifted uncomfortably in my seat as he sat down next to me again.

"What's wrong?"

"My shoulders are killing me from carrying all this heavy shit around all the time."

"Want me to rub you down?"

I raised an eyebrow. "That sounds enticing." My eyes followed him as he stood up and began to lead me over to the bed. "What are you doing?"

"About to give you a real massage. Lay down. I'll be right back."

I hesitated before finally laying on my stomach in the middle of the bed. He briefly returned with baby oil in his hands and knelt down in front of me.

"Take your shirt off."

"Say what now?"

"How else am I supposed to give you a decent massage?"

"Fine." I gruffed and began to take my shirt off but he didn't look away, so I assisted by gently pushing it in the opposite direction. He laughed but didn't say anything. When I was done, I laid back down.

"You done? I can look now?"

"I'm done."

His weight shifted, then cool oil was poured on my back and before it could reach the sheets, his strong, manly hands caught it and ran it up my ribs to my back.

I closed my eyes as he began to gently massage the oil into my skin. His touch made me shiver as he ran his hands down the entirety of my back before focusing his attention to my shoulders. He slid his fingers so carefully, so thoughtfully along the muscles that ran beside my spine, relaxing my body fully.

His thumbs delicately circled on the muscles around my shoulder blades relieving the pressure and pain that were with standing. His fists kneaded all the knots out of my lower back. He painstakingly rubbed, kneaded and soothed my back and shoulders for at least a half an hour to forty-five minutes. Making sure not to miss one spot.

"You feel better?"

"Soooo much better. That was amazing." I rolled over with the blankets still covering my body and looked at his massive, solid structure hovering over me. I caressed his face, and he embraced my hand. "Thank you."

He leaned down and kissed my lips ever so softly. "You are quite welcome Luv."

The both of us laid on the bed staring up at the ceiling spaced out in our own worlds. My hand intertwined in his as he played with my fingers.

"We should have eaten before we drank. My head is spinning right now. Is yours?" he asked.

"No. Not really. But the liquor is burning my stomach."

The covers were still tightly wrapped around my torso as I sat up and looked around.

"What are you looking for?"

"My shirt. I don't know where I threw it."

He too sat up and took his shirt off exposing his sexy bare chest and handed it to me. I couldn't help but to stare. I couldn't resist the temptation. Not this time.

He laid back down and covered his face with his hands as I put the shirt over my head. I held it tightly to me, smelling his scent that was emanating from it.

I stood to my feet and grabbed a few bottles of water and handed him one of which he guzzled down.

"What do you want to eat?" I asked, sipping mine.

"Man. I don't even care. Something sweet."

"Want the last apple? A pear is over there too."

"I don't care Nat." he snapped. Realizing his tone, he retracted his words almost immediately and apologized. "I'm sorry. It's just my head."

The apple was placed near him before I went to grab some pain meds that he took.

"Thanks Babe." he said, again and once again, it caught me by surprise.

The apple was gone in a matter of a few bites and the core was thrown away before I stumbled in the dark to get back to the bed. Out of the darkness, a flashlight came on for me so I could see where I was going. It went back off when I laid at his side with my back firmly pressed against his.

"Do you realize what you're calling me?" I whispered.

I felt him turn and cradle my body before kissing the back of my head.

"I know what I'm calling you."

"Why are you calling me that?"

His warm breath breezed past my neck causing me to quiver and grab his hand firmly almost in a way to say that I wanted him. I did want him, but I tried to suppress the ever-growing desire for him.

"You are my Babe. The name suits you quite well."

Another kiss was placed on my neck before he snuggled up with me like his teddy bear. His grip loosened a bit and his breathing slowed. I was right after him with a big smile on my face.

Inner Demons

A groggy feeling fell over me as I opened my eyes. The sun barked down on my face through a small crack in between the curtain and the window. Quickly, the blanket was pulled up over my head which pounded like a drum. Maureese's arm was still wrapped snugly around my waist and as I tried to move it so I could go to the bathroom, he jerked me back and sat up with a concerned look on his face.

"Are you ok?" he muttered.

"I'm fine. I just have to tinkle is all."

He let me go, yawned and stretched. "My bad."

The room was frigid as I tiptoed my way to the bathroom. On my way back, I turned the heater on before getting back in the bed where his warmth awaited me.

"My head hurts now." I complained.

"Mine still does too and that sunlight is fuckin killin me." He threw a piece of clothing at the window causing the curtain to fall to the floor. The sun smiled at our pain before we both threw the covers over our faces.

"Way to go Reese." I muffled.

"Hush."

He kissed my cheek before he went to the bathroom himself. When he came back, he had food and water in his hands, some of which he handed to me. We sat Indian style under the blankets and ate side by side.

"I want to start a garden." I randomly said.

"Winter is coming. How are we going to grow anything?"

"It's amazing. They have these things called pots that you can grow plants in." I said in a very sarcastic manner. He paused before laughing at my words.

I looked down at the food in my hand. "Ugh. I don't even want this."

He snatched it from me. "I'll eat it."

"Hey!" I whined as he shoved the whole damn thing in his mouth. "Well damn."

"I'm hungry. This fruit shit is not cutting it for me. I'm a big dude."

"Big indeed. How tall are you anyway?"

"Six- five, six-six last time I checked."

I raised my eyebrows. "Well damn."

"How tall are you shorty?"

"I'm five foot nine thank you very much."

"You're still a shorty."

"Oh whatever." I grabbed a water bottle and chugged it down. He looked at me in amazement. "What? I was thirsty."

"Yea, I see."

"Glad I'm not hungry!"

"There's more food in there. Don't even start."

I looked up through the window where the sun was burning bright in the sky and pointed to it as I spoke. "Can you fix the damn curtain please? If I wasn't hung over, I wouldn't mind but that shit is in the way right now."

"I will. Don't worry." He was so nonshalant about it.

"You're such a jerk today." I teased.

"I'm in a good mood."

"So you turn into an ass when you're in a good mood?"

He rubbed his stomach and made a face before getting up. "I gotta take a shit man."

I burst out laughing. "Way too much information Reese."

"I do though. My stomach fuckin hurts."

When he disappeared in the bathroom, I laid back down and cuddled up and buried deep inside the covers still smelling his scent from both the covers and the shirt. It was a strong and masculine scent that I could literally smell all day long and be quite content about it.

The room soon grew darker, and I peeped my head out to find him putting the curtain back up. My head was still spinning as I drank a little of the water from last night. It helped a little, but not as much as I wanted it to.

"You feel better?"

"Much. So what about this garden now? What will you grow?"

"Herbs for now. Fruits and vegetables maybe."

"No shit you don't say. What kind of fruits and vegetables woman?"

"The kind you eat." He looked at me and realized I was messing with him too.

"Great, forget your garden. Good luck with that." he said, turning away from me in a playful manner.

"No, no, no, I'm done, I'm done." I joked turning him to face me once again. He was dangerously close to me as he rested his weight on his forearms. "I was thinking lettuce, tomatoes, onions, peppers, fresh herbs… Stuff like that."

"Where would you set up the pots and stuff?"

"Under the windows. Get better curtain rods so we can actually look out the windows during the day and close them at night." I closed my eyes and winced.

"Does your head still hurt?"

"No, not that much. I'm just still really tired."

"You going to sleep?"

"Yea, probably. What about you?" My voice grew faint each time I spoke.

"Yea, I'll be joining you soon." Him softly rubbing my arms is all that I could remember for I fell back asleep.

"Nat! Natalie! Babe, Wake up!" Reese yelled, shaking me.

I sat up and looked around the dimly lit room. My clothes were damp with sweat and my breathing was heavy. Our eyes met as he sat hovered over me. The sweat that had accumulated on my forehead was wiped away.

"What happened?"

"You were screaming. You have a nightmare?"

Tears formed in my eyes as I began to remember parts of the dream I was having, and I buried my face in his chest. He held me tight stroking my hair.

"I remember watching those things tear my family apart, then they started chasing after me. I was running as fast as I could, but it seemed like I was moving in slow motion. They got me Reese. They got me." I cried.

"Shhhh. They didn't get you. They won't get you." He began to slowly rock side to side trying to get me to relax. "It's ok Baby. It's ok. Look at me." He grabbed my face with both hands, wiped my tears and stared me in my eyes. "It's ok. Nothing is going to happen to you."

I placed my head back on his chest and sniffled. My eyes felt red and puffy once the tears stopped streaming down my face. He pulled away from me and returned with a tissue that he used to dry my face with.

"I can get it Reese, I got it. Thank you."

He sat next to me with his arm around my shoulder. I could feel him looking at me, but I turned away.

"You feel better now?"

"I feel ugly now."

"What? Why?"

"My face is all puffy." I sniffled again as the tears welled up in my eyes.

"You are still beautiful to me even with your puffy chunk, chunk face. You'll always be beautiful. So cut that shit out. And stop crying Nat. I don't like when you cry." He pulled me closer to him and I rested my head on his shoulder. "You hungry?"

"No."

"You haven't eaten anything all day. You gotta eat."

"I'm not hungry." I pulled away from him and laid back down with my back facing him. He tried to hold me like he usually did, but I pulled away and pushed him back.

"What's wrong?" He sounded a bit upset.

"I don't want to be held right now Maureese." I snapped.

He got out of bed. "Fine." he said, sternly and went to sit in the chair after grabbing some food for himself.

As he ate, I laid there silently to myself staring at the wooden wall in front of me with the dream still heavy on my mind. The covers were pulled close for comfort as the gruesome dream replayed over and over again in my head.

Several hours had passed and still not one word was exchanged between us. The light went off and he joined me in the bed with his back facing towards me. I could tell he wanted to hold me, but he didn't.

Silently I cried to myself hoping he wouldn't hear. This time, I don't know why I was sad or upset, I just… Was. It could be that we weren't holding each other. It could have been the predicament the world was in at the moment. What life was right now. Fear of my dream coming true like so many of the others had done.

Fear of uncertainty. Fear of the unknown. Whatever it was, I wanted it to stop, so I eliminated one of the possibilities. The one that bothered me the most at this moment. I turned over and wrapped him in my arms. He grabbed them and caressed them but still didn't say a word to me. So, I spoke first.

"Are you mad at me?"

There was a moment of silence before he responded. "Why would I be mad at you Natalie?" he said, quietly and firmly.

"From earlier. How I pulled away from you."

He hesitated again. "I mean, I felt some type of way. I don't know why you did it, but I'm not mad at you."

"K." I simply said softly. Soon after, I heard his breathing get deeper and he stopped caressing my arm. I knew he was asleep, leaving me to fight my inner demons alone.

I wanted to tell him my thoughts but didn't want to seem like a nag or… or… someone who complained and worried too much. But the other part of me knew he would want me to talk to him about it and not bottle it up. But I had already agreed with myself to keep it to myself. Sort things out on my own.

I got up and turned the lamp back on. The cabin was still warm from when the heater was on earlier, and I went over and grabbed my poison to help soothe my pain. A different poison that I knew I shouldn't be drinking, but I grabbed it anyway. The bottle of Henny.

I sat in my chair and sipped on it slowly and let the feeling take over me. But instead of making things better, it made it worse. My mind started flashing back to all the negative aspects of my life. First at the past week that I endured with these creatures from hell and all the corpses rotting in the streets. I drank some more. Then to the woman who was slain right in front of me. Then, my mind sank deeper into my past and the horrific days that were casted upon me.

The people that I had been living with and all the bullshit they had put me through. I drank more. The man that had shattered my childhood and my innocence. I drank more. Then, it went even further back to when I lost my parents. I drank more and began to cry again.

The bathroom door closed and locked after I entered. In my drunken slumber, I began to throw things from the cabinet and take my anger out on the walls. Eventually, I let the pain out and began to scream. The type of screams from a nightmare. The type of screams that roared and were overwhelmed with anger along with sadness and hurt.

Finally, I began to calm down and sat on the closed toilet seat for a while sobbing uncontrollably, hugging myself. The negative thoughts swirled in my head non-stop. My sides hurt. My eyes hurt. My throat burned from the liquor and screaming. I wiped my face and my eyes and stared at myself in the mirror. My eyes were puffier than earlier. I absolutely hated crying, so, I usually avoided it altogether. My deepest pain was locked away, but when I did let it out, it was usually this outcome. Minus the throwing and beating of the walls of course. That was the Henny's doing.

Composing myself, I opened the door and proceeded to walk out when I saw Reese sitting, leaned up against the wall. He looked up at me and slowly stood to his feet when I came out. He walked up and examined me from my face to my bleeding and sliced up hands. I hadn't even noticed.

My hands were placed under cool water and cleaned up before I was guided to my chair where he sat me down. A bottle of water was handed to me before he grabbed a clean washcloth that was used to wipe my face free of the sweat and tears. I sniffled and watched blankly as he cleaned my hands up with alcohol and, although I felt the burn, I didn't flinch. My body was numb all over.

Eventually, I grabbed the water and held it to my mouth to drink but he had to tip it up to assist me. I absolutely felt helpless. I attempted to stand up. "Where are you going?" he asked.

"I have to pee."

With his assistance, I got to my feet and headed to the bathroom. Before I could make it, I tripped over nothing and fell flat on my stomach on the hard floor.

"Come on Nat." He sounded aggravated as he helped me up and the rest of the way to the bathroom.

"I got it from here." I slurred and pushed him back. Kinda. He didn't really budge, but he left me on my own.

The bathroom was in complete chaos from my actions. After using the bathroom, I stumbled out and fell right into his strong arms where he carried me to the bed and laid me down.

My head was spinning, and I felt a strong headache coming on. As I shifted uncomfortably, Reese went to clean up the mess I had made. When he was done, he handed me a few slices of bread.

"Here. This should soak up some of the liquor." He turned and walked away as I nibbled on the bread slices.

"Reese."

"Yes?" he asked sternly, coming back to my side.

"Can I have something for my headache? My head hurts."

"No. You drank way too much."

I sighed as he walked away from me again. Closing my eyes offered no relief as I tried to force myself to sleep. Nausea and the headache was slowly creeping up on me and I took a few more bites of the bread. It made me feel a little better, but at the end of the day, I still felt like shit emotionally and physically. Only time would make me feel better. Physically anyway and I had to wait it out and suffer while the alcohol ran its course in my system.

He pulled his chair over to where I was laying and sat down where he watched me. He tried to read me. Probably was wondering what the hell was wrong with me and if he had asked, I wouldn't have an answer to give.

Another cool washcloth was placed on my forehead before he stroked my hair gently.

"How are you feeling?"

"Like shit Reese."

He held up the bottle I was drinking from. "I can imagine." The bottle twisted as he examined it. "You drank damn near half the bottle. What were you thinking?"

I turned away. "I don't want to talk about it."

He exhaled deeply. Frustrated again. "Well, I'm here when you're ready to talk. I hope you know that. You can talk to me about anything."

"Thank you." I whispered.

"Tell me though. Was it something that I did?"

I turned and looked at him. "It wasn't anything that you did." The washcloth was replaced over my face, and it offered great relief to my swollen eyes. "I'm sorry Luv. I'm so sorry."

He rubbed my shoulder trying to comfort me. "You don't have to be sorry."

"I don't know what's wrong with me." My voice began to shake, and I felt the tears coming back.

"Don't cry Babe. Talk to me. What's going on?"

"I don't know what to say. I have so much on my mind. I tried to drink it away thinking it would make it better, but it only made it worse."

"But why'd you drink the Henny though? You told me it made you angry and reckless." He paused. "Did you drink it on purpose?"

"Maybe. I don't know."

"Don't drink it anymore. Understand?"

"I won't."

"It's like you want to self-destruct and I don't know why. I was so scared when you were in the bathroom screaming like that. Throwing things. I couldn't get to you. I couldn't help you. I don't like that."

"I'm sorry." I whispered after some time had passed.

"Get some rest now Luv. I know you're tired."

The lights went off before he laid down with his back to me and we laid like that for a while, but I wanted his touch. Needed his hug. His warmth. His embrace.

"Can you hold me?"

Without hesitation, he turned to face me. His face in mine. "Babe, your breath smells like hot ass liquor." I felt his strong hold on me before I blew my breath in his face. "Really though?"

"Payback's a bitch." I slurred before I giggled slightly. I felt his tongue lick my entire forehead and his laughter erupted from the darkness.

"Really? You're lucky I'm fucked up over here or I'd get you back."

"You ain't gon do shit."

"Wait til morning. Imma get you back." He kissed my lips slowly. "Mmm. Don't do that."

"Hush and go to sleep Babe."

The Radio

The sun was high up in the sky again before I woke up the next day. My head still hurt, and my vision was still blurry, but I wasn't nauseous. That was a relief. Reese was still sleeping next to me, and I stood up quietly trying not to disturb him before I went to the bathroom. I looked around, and it was as if nothing had happened last night. Guilt over took me for having to make him clean up after me last night.

My hands were swollen and torn up and burned as I tried to wash them. I looked at myself in the mirror as I brushed my teeth. The swelling was still there, but not nearly as bad as last night.

"Nat, I gotta take a piss." he said, out of nowhere from the other side of the door. I didn't even hear him walk up.

After I finished brushing my teeth, the door opened, and I proceeded to walk out but he was in the way blocking the door.

"What? Move."

He bent down to give me a kiss and I met him half way before he let me walk past him. I still felt very groggy as I went into the kitchen to find something to eat and when I did, I literally had to force it down. I chugged an entire bottle of water afterwards to get rid of my hangover hydration.

"How are you holding up over there?" he asked, grabbing the rest of my orange.

"I don't think I'll be drinking for a while." I looked through the cabinets trying to find something else that looked appetizing but found something that sparked my interest instead. I had forgotten it was stowed away as I grabbed it and brought it over to my chair.

"You think we'll hear anything interesting on it?" he asked, sitting next to me.

"Maybe we can find out more of what's going on."

I struggled with the package before he took it from me and opened it with ease. I glared at him for his strength as he put the batteries in and scanned for a clear channel. For the most part, all we heard was static before the faint sound of a woman's voice began to come through. She was barely audible from all the chaos that was in her background, but we listened for a half hour and got an idea of what she was saying.

So far, well populated areas were affected. We were told that the government wasn't going to disclose what was causing the destruction and that the military had everything under control. We were advised to stay indoors, and help would be on the way.

She began to go through a long list of major areas that had been hit. She began to name place after place in the United States at first. Next, she began to name places worldwide. As she began to go down the list, we felt the house rumble ever so slightly. Maureese grabbed my leg as we both sat straight up in our seats.

"What was that?" My heart was racing. Before he could answer, the house shook again uncontrollably. Much stronger and closer this time and I grabbed his hand firmly. "Reese, I'm scared."

I looked him in his eyes, and he looked into mine. He looked confused and scared at the same time. I opened my mouth to speak but was stopped.

"Shhh..." he said, sharply. The house shook again. The trembles had the whole cabin shaking ferociously for moments at a time. Every second it seemed to be getting closer and longer.

"Turn the radio off." Maureese whispered as. I quickly pulled the batteries out. The female's voice faded away.

Another tremble came for a longer period of time, then stopped suddenly and went in another direction. Over a period of ten minutes of not moving and barely breathing, the trembles slowly diminished in the distance.

I loosened my grip on his hand and began to breathe normally after a half hour had passed.

"Why the fuck was it out here?"

"I haven't felt it that close since the first night."

He sat and thought for a minute before standing up. "Hand me the radio."

"Where are you going?"

"Nat, just hand me the damn radio. And the batteries."

What he was asking for was placed in his hands and he began to walk to the door and put his boots on.

I sprang up to where he was and blocked the door with my body. "What are you doing?"

"I'm going to test a theory."

"No you're not."

His gun holster and a few knives were put on his hip. "Nat, get out of the way."

"I'm going with you."

Before I could put my first boot on he stopped me and pushed me over to the bed. "No. You're not. You're staying here."

He walked back to the door but before he could get there, I was blocking it again. "I'm going with you." I repeated hoping his mind had changed, but it was already made up.

My arm was gripped firmly as I was led back over to the bed. "Stay here." he demanded sternly.

Sadly, I sat there watching him put on the rest of his gear before walking over to him once more with no intention to stop his stubborn ass.

A kiss was placed on my forehead as the door opened and he cautiously looked out. "I'll be right back. I promise." The door closed and I watched him disappear from the window into the thick of the woods.

My eyes brimmed with tears as I kept telling myself he would be alright and that he would be back. I paced back and forth in the cabin, waiting for him to return, wishing he had never gone out there in the first place. Wishing he would have allowed me to at least go with him.

I needed something to do to distract my ever-wandering mind, so I decided to clean up the cabin. But I found myself looking out the window every so often to see if he was on his way back and was disappointed when I didn't see his familiar figure coming towards the house.

My mouth was parched so I grabbed a bottle of water, but before I could pour the cold liquid in my mouth, the house began to tremble and shake uncontrollably. Instantly, I froze up and feared for the worst. That something had happened to him. That something was coming here.

The trembling stopped. Another few minutes passed, and it continued steadily before it stopped again. Each time, it caused the cabin to sway a bit and made the windows clatter together. I crept over to the window and peered out hoping to see something. Anything. But what I saw only terrified me and made me fear for his safety.

In the distance, trees were twisted and toppled over in a path of devastation in the same direction Maureese had gone in. The earth beneath them had simply crumbled and there was nothing I could do but wait even though there was so much more I wanted to do.

The minutes melted into an hour and still I waited for Reese to come back. The sun was beginning to set, and my knees were growing weak from fear as I kept looking through the hazy windows and not seeing signs of him. I didn't know what to do or what to think or expect. My stomach growled and the cabin grew colder as the darkness began to take over. The heater was turned on but that was only because it was right by my feet.

Once I could no longer see outside, the lamp was turned on and I sat on the bed wrapped in the covers as I slowly nibbled at my food. I was beginning to worry that something had happened to him. Trying to decide if I should go out and search for him. but where would I begin? I tried to shake the negative thoughts, but they kept coming back.

Finally, the door creaked open, and he came in. The covers were thrown off my shoulders and I jumped into his arms with excitement and relief. He held my weight for a while and kissed me before putting me down and taking off his outside clothes. As he sat in his chair, I brought him some water that he chugged down.

He washed his hands in the kitchen before collapsing in the bed with his arms held out for me to join him. I did happily and inhaled his scent as he played in my hair.

"What happened Babe? I was so worried about you. I saw the trees collapse in the direction you went. The house shook like crazy. Did you see what it was?" I rambled. He caressed my face as he stared up at the ceiling.

"I didn't see what it was, but I saw the ground collapse right in front of me. It responded to the radio transmission like I thought. When I turned it on, it could pinpoint me with direct accuracy, but when I turned it off, it stopped in its tracks. I moved to a different spot in a different direction and walked and yelled, it moved slowly, but as soon as I turned the radio on, it looked like it would roll in the ground, then come barreling after me.

I stood still for about 10 minutes trying to figure out what to do next. Then, I took off running through the woods mad far away from here. I turned the radio on and left it and watched to see what it would do. It basically collapsed the earth and sucked the damn radio right up and crushed it. When it did, it disappeared back into the ground. Then I came back." He looked down at me. I sat up and looked at him. "How are you? Are you ok?"

"I am now. Just hungry." He began to get up. "Where are you going?"

"To get us something to eat. I'm hungry too."

"Sit down and relax." I demanded. "I can get it. What do you want?"

"Doesn't matter." He chuckled as I scavenged the cabinets.

Once I made a selection for the both of us and opened the cans, I walked back over to where he was already sitting up and waiting. As usual, he gulfed his food down before I could even get my first few bites in.

I drank a bit of my pineapple juice, and as I did, a few of my pineapples quickly disappeared from my plate. I heard him happily chewing as I looked at him like he was crazy.

"Really Reese?"

"What?" He played it off and did it again. All I could really do was watch as my pineapples slowly disappeared off my plate and into his mouth.

"Reese!" I shouted in disbelief that he would be so bold to continue to eat more.

"I just had to do a quality check for you. Make sure they were good enough for you to eat."

"You're so full of shit." I laughed.

"Yea, so?" He went to take the empty cans and plates to the kitchen, but I stopped him.

"I got it Babe. Leave it there and relax."

He looked at me shocked and a bit delighted. "What did you call me?"

I looked back at him confused, not exactly sure of what he was referring to. Then it hit me. "… Did I call you Babe?"

"Wasn't the first time either."

"I'm sorry. I was so scared of what might have happened to you..."

"You don't have to explain yourself or apologize."

While I took our things into the kitchen, I thought back on my word choice. Why did I call him Babe? Did I really mean it or was it just the fact that he was gone, and I was worried about him? Was I really falling for this man? But how could I in such a short amount of time?

"Nat, can you turn the heat off? I'm burning the fuck up." His shirt soon came off exposing his bare skin.

"Yea. I can uhh... I can turn it off." I choked over my words and tried not to stare too hard as the heater went off and a few candles were lit. The candle light flickered as I went back to where he was laying and sat down next to him on the bed.

The dim light of the candle glowed off his muscular, moist body and I found myself staring shyly at him. I wanted to touch him so bad, and I guess my thoughts relayed on my face because he spoke out.

"You can touch if you want. I'm not gonna bite... Unless you want me to." he flirted in a deep voice.

Timidly, I reached my hand out and caressed his skin softly. My fingers slowly slid down the definition of his eight pack before rolling down to his prominent lower obliques. They swirled around on his body tenderly before my nails dragged gently across it.

He began to laugh slightly, and I pulled away. "That tickles man."

"Sorry." I smiled and continued to caress him.

A soft kiss was placed on his abs before I laid down at his side. He sat up and hovered over me before coming up to my face where his lips timidly met mine. But this kiss was different. He didn't pull away like he usually did, and all his weight was placed on me. As our lips locked, my eyes closed, and the kiss grew more intense. Our breathing intensified.

My arms wrapped around his neck as his hands explored the contours of my body. My breasts fit perfectly in his hands as he softly stroked and played with my nipples. I let out a soft moan of delight which only caused him to kiss me more intensely. The sensations he was giving me caused my body to writhe under him. Slowly, his hands made their way down my abs and to my wet temple that was elated by his touch and throbbed and begged him to penetrate.

I came to my senses and pulled away from him even though I didn't fully want to. "Reese. I can't." I interrupted and pushed him back slightly. I allowed him to kiss me one more time before pulling away again. "Reese. I can't."

He stopped and buried his face in my chest. "I know, I'm sorry."

"Don't be sorry. I'm sorry." A few deep breaths were taken trying to calm my intense desire to be with him. For him to finish what he started.

"You're just... so... sexy. I couldn't help myself."

"You are too..." My voice trailed off. "I can't..."

"You don't have to explain yourself. I understand. But FUCK." He smothered me in kisses before rolling off me and staring back up at the ceiling.

The back of my hand was brought to his juicy lips and was held there for a while before it was brought down and placed on his chest which was beating just as fast as mine. Both of us were out of breath even though nothing physical had taken place. From sheer passion and lust we both had for each other.

I was so pissed at myself for stopping him and half of me wanted to keep going. I wanted him so bad I could practically feel him inside me. Pleasuring me. Satisfying and quenching my thirst that I had for him. But I couldn't bring myself to do it. Not yet anyway. As I took another breath, I wondered what he would feel like.

I rolled over on my side sexually frustrated, and he didn't make it any better when he held me from behind and I could feel his hard dick press up against my cheek. Although he tried to position himself so that it wouldn't poke me, it still did and I giggled.

"It's not funny." he whispered jokingly.

"I'm in the same boat as you."

"Go to sleep woman before I come for more." He bit my neck and turned away from me.

"Why did you move?"

"I'm tempted to touch."

My position shifted and my arms wrapped around him. Even though I was tempted, I resisted the urge to explore his body further. Why would I tease and start the both of us back up?

Where I'm Not Wanted

Reese was fully dressed the next morning and him rustling in the kitchen is what woke me up. His bags were packed, and he was geared up like he was about to go on a run.

"Good morning sleepy head."

"Good morning. Where are you going?" I asked in a groggy voice.

"I'm going to get more food from the grocery store. I'm trying to get as much as I can before it starts really getting cold." He put one last thing in his bag before walking over to put his boots on.

"You're going by yourself? Why didn't you wake me up?"

"Cuz you were knocked the fuck out."

"I want to go with you though. I always want to go with you." I whined.

"Get dressed then." he said, with a mild tone. It seemed as though something was bothering him.

I slowly sat up. "What's wrong? Were you really gonna just leave? Did you eat yet? How long have you been up?" I rambled on.

"Nat, please with the questions." He sat down in the chair, and I looked at him confused before moving closer to analyze his emotions.

"Reese, what's wrong?"

"Nothing. I'm just ready to go. It's still early and I want to get this shit done."

"What are you trying to do? We have so much already."

He gave me a blank stare. "I want to clear out the store and get as much food as we possibly can get from there. All that food is just sitting there when we could have it here for ourselves. I don't want to go hungry this winter."

My clothes and gear were tossed on as I spoke. "Why didn't you tell me this before?"

"Because I know how you are. I didn't want you to talk me out of it."

"...out of what?"

"Taking it all for ourselves. You would want me to leave some for other people, correct?"

He definitely had a point there. I didn't answer, just hung my head low. "You still could have told me." I solemnly said.

"Just... Come on. I can use your help to knock this out."

An emergency bag was packed for me as my boots slid on my feet. On the way out, I looked at him once more trying to figure him out.

"What's on your mind?" I asked one last time as we began walking.

"Nothing." he simply replied and walked ahead of me. I guess he had inner demons that he was trying to fight off too. Hopefully, he would feel better as the day progressed.

No words were spoken on the entire walk to the plaza, and he stayed a few paces ahead of me. His walk was brisk and it seemed to be full of anger and frustration. I just let him go. I knew the way and he didn't seem like he wanted to be bothered at all. The beautiful sights of nature kept my mind preoccupied instead of wondering what was going on in his.

Before we entered, he scoped out the place to ensure we were alone and when he was sure we were he came back and got me.

"What's the game plan here?"

"Fill the carts up with as much food as possible or anything you think we could use. Same as it always is." His tone was dark.

I stood there for a minute before walking up behind him and spinning him around by his shoulder.

"What the hell is wrong with you?" I barked. "You've been acting weird all fuckin day."

The look on his face was blank as he stared at me, then away, then back at me. "I just needed some alone time to clear my head. I'm just thinking of some shit and trying to work some things out in my mind. I'm just feeling a little bit down is all. Is that alright with you?"

"Why wouldn't you just say that in the first place? If you needed alone time, why even ask me to come along with you?"

"You wanted to come."

"Well, I don't want to be where I'm not wanted." I huffed and began to walk away. My feelings were hurt, yes, but I completely understood what he meant.

Before I could get too far away, my arm was grabbed, and I was turned to face him. "Nat, it's not like that at all. You know I love your company just sometimes... I need to be alone."

"Then you should have said that before we left." I said shaking free from his grasp and walking away.

"Then you would have been pissed like you are now."

I turned back to him. "I'm not pissed. You should have just spoke your mind from the jump. Let's just get what we need and get out of here. I'll give you your space."

Although he didn't say anything back, I could feel his eyes on me as I walked away with my cart. On the opposite side of the store, I began grabbing up things I thought we would both like until my bags and cart were full. There were still so many items left on the shelves as I made my way back to the front and I wasn't sure how he planned on clearing the entire place out. Where would we even store all of it?

"You ready to head back?" he asked in a mellow voice. I responded with a head nod and began to leave. "Nat." his voice bellowed out, stopping me in my tracks. I turned around to see what he wanted. "I didn't mean to…"

"Don't worry about it Maureese." I interrupted and began walking again.

I didn't know what to say to him. Didn't know how to feel. Just wanted to go back home. To do what? I don't know. Just wanted to go back and put this whole day behind us.

When we arrived at the cabin, the carts were unloaded. Once again, the entire walk home was silent as well as bringing everything in the house. I really did want to talk to him and joke around with him like we usually did, but he still seemed down and out so I let it be.

"I'm going back to get more stuff." He finally said breaking the silence, but I remained quiet as I looked up at him. "You can come if you want."

His words were almost contradicting, like he was torn in two. It was as if he was trying to please me and make me feel happy while at the same time needing and wanting his alone time.

"You can go while I put this stuff away and clean up." I tried to put it in a way that wouldn't make him feel guilty about leaving me by myself. I was torn too. I wanted to go help my partner in any way possible, but helping might just be to stay here and let him sort out whatever he was going through on his own.

"You sure Nat? I don't mind."

"I'm sure Reese. Go ahead."

He gave me a hug and a kiss on my forehead before I watched him disappear through the woods. I admired him as he left. I studied his walk. The way he moved. The way he carried himself. A smile fell over my face as I blushed and felt giddy. When he came back, I hope he would be in a much better mood than when he left. I also hoped he would come back quickly and safely.

A few hours had passed and there was still no sign of him. In that time, everything we had gotten on the run was stored away and the cabin was cleaned fully from the kitchen to the bathroom. Swept, mopped and wiped down. Every now and then… ok, quite often, I looked out the window to see if he was coming.

While I waited for him to return, I sat and ate some canned fruit in the chair. I peered out the window one last time when I went to wash and throw away the can and I finally saw his familiar figure walking towards the house pushing a very full cart with a very heft bag on his shoulders.

I was elated and ran out the cabin greeting him with a big hug which caused him to drop the bag. His embrace was warm, and I didn't realize just how much I missed him until I was wrapped up in his arms and inhaling his scent.

"Well hello to you too. Miss me much?" His voice was much brighter than before.

"I did! I didn't realize how much I would." The bag that had fallen to the ground was picked up and slung over my shoulder. "Are you feeling better now?"

We both began walking to the house. "I'm feeling better." There was a slight pause before he spoke again. "I missed you too." It was almost as if he was realizing just how much he missed me as well.

A smile spread across my face, but I didn't turn around to look at him. The smile, however, remained there the entire time we unloaded the cart, bringing everything inside. The newly cleaned cabin was once again cluttered. This time, as I tried to put things away, it was much harder due to the fact that there wasn't anywhere to put it all. But we made it work and the cabin was clean once again.

"Did you clean it out to your satisfaction?"

"Not at all but I think we have more than enough for now. We can't even fit all the shit in the cabinets." He paused and looked around. "You cleaned in here?"

I giggled. "I told you I was going to. Swept, mopped, all that."

"You're missing one thing though." He moved into the kitchen and lit a few candles before coming back to me and playing in my hair while admiring me. "I'm going to go take a shower. I'm beat for the day."

"You want me to make you something to eat?"

"Sure, some soup would be nice. Thanks."

"Potato?"

"Potato." he reassured me and walked into the bathroom with his things.

There was nothing left for me to do while I waited for his food to warm up, so I just sat down in the chair bored as hell. Usually, my thoughts would be swirling around in my mind but, for some reason, my mind was drawing a blank. No thoughts passed through. Good or bad. I was finally at peace. For now anyway and it was a relief.

When he came out of the bathroom, he was fully dressed to my surprise, and he sat down next to me. "You look bored."

"I'm very bored. Your food should be done by now."

He grabbed it off the heater while I handed him a spoon from the kitchen. "Thanks Babe. You not hungry?"

"I ate earlier. I'm good."

I sat back down in my chair not really knowing what to say to him. Not really knowing where his mind was at, at the moment but I still wanted to be near him. Whenever he wasn't close, I would always be wondering if he was alright and honestly, I would miss him a great deal.

"You ok?"

"Yea, I'm fine. Are you alright?"

"You are so quiet. Just wondering is all. I'm so tired. I'm gonna take it down."

I rubbed his shoulder. "You should get some rest then. You did a lot today."

"Not really. Didn't feel like it anyway. You aren't tired?" he asked, finishing off his soup and throwing his can away.

"No, not really. I'm just… chill I guess you can say."

"Wanna lay with me?" he asked timidly.

"I have to take a shower first."

I stood up and stretched as he came over to where I was and looked down at me before pulling me in close. His soft lips touched mine and his touch was firm and inviting. My arms wrapped around his neck as our kiss grew from caring to passionate in no time and the next thing I knew, we were feeling up on each other.

I felt myself get warm, wet and ready for his penetration. The both of us wanted each other so bad and I couldn't understand why we teased each other so. More or less, it was me that was holding back, but that was fading quickly.

I began to back up with him still wrapped in my arms and he had no choice but to follow. It was almost like I wanted to pull away, but at the same time, I didn't want him to stop. I felt myself press up against the counter where he lifted me up on it. My legs were wrapped around his waist.

He stopped kissing me and stared down at me who had a hard time, yet again, looking him in the eyes. His hands grabbed my face and tried to bring it up to his, but I buried it in his shirt. He laughed and kissed me one last time before lifting me off the counter.

"Go take your shower Babe." he said, in a low, sexy tone.

The cold shower shocked me back to normal before I got dressed and joined him in the bed with nothing but underwear and a t-shirt on. It was as if I was inviting him into my temple. Setting myself up for the pleasure I wanted and didn't want at the same time. I was conflicted with myself but why was I holding back?

I was so sure that he was asleep as I snuggled in next to him until he rolled over on his back and caressed my body sending chills down my spine. I quivered. My head rested on his chest, and I listened to his steady breathing and heartbeat as the silence of the room engulfed us.

The two of us laid there, not saying a word to each other, yet communicating in another way. Caressing each other softly. Not in a sexual manner but in a loving one as if we were getting to know one another on a whole new level. Neither one of us pulled away and we let the moment happen. Let the energy between us flow freely and I loved every minute of it.

The Truck

The next morning, I was awakened by warm kisses being placed on my cheek. My eyes slowly opened, and I saw a very handsome Maureese smiling in front of me.

"Good morning beautiful."

I couldn't help but to smile and blush a bit. "Good morning handsome man." My arms wrapped around him, giving him a big hug. The sun was still low in the sky as I peered at it through the crack in the curtain. The day was still young and there was so much that needed to be done. But oh how I wanted to bask in this moment all day.

When I returned from the bathroom, he was already dressed and ready to start the day.

"We need to wash clothes. I'm running low on just about everything."

"Do we have detergent? I don't remember getting any."

"I don't think so." He laughed slightly as he looked through some of our things. "Washing clothes by hand is something I never imagined I'd have to do."

"Me either. I don't think we have any though. We're going to have to get some. Are you really almost out of clean clothes?"

"Almost. I still have a few more clean drawls down in there."

"I'm assuming we're going out soon?"

"The earlier the better. I wanted to go look at a few new places today. See what's around. See what we can get. I was waiting for you to wake up, but you were taking forever, so I helped." A contagious smile spread across his face before he kissed my forehead on the way to the bathroom.

My clothes were thrown on and when he came out of the bathroom, my teeth were brushed. The only thing that I had to do was gear up and put my boots on.

The air was cool as we walked in a different direction than we normally went in. Every so often, he would stop and engrave something on the trees so we could find our way back home. When I looked closely at the engravings, I saw that it was our initials and for some reason, it melted my heart.

We walked for several hours in the tree line that followed the road until we came upon another small shopping plaza. None of the stores really caught our attention except for one. Another hardware store. Before we went down, we watched the surrounding area for a while ensuring that nothing or no one was down there.

When we felt it was safe, we made our way down to the store. This is usually where Reese would do his rounds, but the place was so large, we both proceeded in cautiously together.

The place was in turmoil. Worse than I had ever seen at our other plaza. Almost all of the items were thrown off the now barren shelves and the floors were cluttered in broken and misplaced items.

We both gave each other a look and we both knew what that look meant. Be on high alert. Up and down the aisles we quickly walked to see if there was anything of grave importance that we needed. We didn't want to stay in there any longer than was necessary so if we could get it at the other plaza, we left it in its place.

The biggest slap in the face is when we came to an aisle lined with high end washers and dryers. Free for the taking but had no way of using them. We did find and grab some detergent and fabric softener along with a portable washing machine that would alleviate some of the work of washing clothes by hand.

I turned the corner and stopped causing him to bump right into me. My eyes were fixated on something that we could really use. A shit load of propane tanks were there in our faces but how the hell were we going to get them home?

He grabbed my hand and drug me along. I had no choice but to follow, but of course, I had to ask. "Where are we going?"

"To get a truck."

I slowed down and he slowed down with me. "Wait... What? Do you not remember what happened to the last vehicle we saw in the woods?"

"The grave diggers are only attracted to sound waves."

"That's what we think... Reese, I'm not sure about this."

"There's only one way to find out. We need those tanks and there's no way in hell I'm going to lug them back and forth to the house. We need this truck Babe."

"Reese, this is crazy."

"What's crazy is not even trying. I'll take the radio out then there shouldn't be a problem."

I stopped and stared at him hoping he would change his mind. "This is too dangerous."

"Imagine if this works though Babe. Imagine all the stores we can hit up. All the things we could get."

He sounded so hopeful, and I couldn't break his spirit. Even though I hated this idea, I reluctantly gave in and walked again. "We can try it and if even the slightest fuckin movement comes, that's it."

"It's gonna work. I need it to work."

There were a few sets of keys for the rental trucks outside and we grabbed them all hoping one would be to a flatbed. One by one, the keys were tried for the flatbed until the door finally unlocked and he opened it. But that wasn't the part that troubled us.

The entire radio console of the truck was pulled out before we took a deep breath and started it up. Both of us stepped back and listened carefully for a few minutes to ensure we didn't draw unwanted attention from our actions. To our surprise, nothing came.

"Get in the truck Babe!" he yelled, opening the door for me. I got in and slid to the other side while he got in, put the gear in drive and we headed to the front of the store.

The truck turned off and we worked diligently to get all the propane heaters off the shelves, onto a flatbed cart and to the front of the store where they were unloaded onto the truck. As he loaded them, I secured them with bungee cords and moving blankets to make sure they wouldn't slide around or clink together. Everything else we had grabbed from the store, plus a few extra items were loaded on top and we pulled away.

"Holy shit, I can't believe it's working." He exclaimed as we drove up the hill and into the familiar woods.

"Just watch where you're going. Don't hit anything." I said with a smile.

All the tanks were unloaded and stored in the basement when we got back. Although the task was hard and a pain in the ass, it sure beat the hell out of having to lug all of them back to the house. Especially at such a far distance.

"What are you going to do with this truck Babe?" We can't leave it here. It could draw unwanted attention." I said to him a bit worried.

"Honestly, I want to go get as much stuff as we can. Get all the food, all the tanks at the other plaza."

"Fine. But when we're done, put this shit somewhere and leave it."

He chuckled a bit as he opened my door to let me in. Once he was in, we drove to our usual plaza and damn near cleared the place out. Same with the camping store grabbing any and everything we thought we would need now or later.

The last store we went into was the hardware store where we grabbed the rest of the tanks that were there. While he grabbed the ones from the back, I was tasked at grabbing the few that were left on the shelf. The first three were taken down just fine, but the fourth one was a bit of a struggle and on the fifth and last one, my arms began to give out on me before I had a full grasp of the tank. It was way above my head and was slowly sliding off the shelf before I had a full grip of it. I began to panic.

"Reese!" I hollered hoping he could hear me from the back. The more time that elapsed, the further it was sliding and the heavier it was getting. "Reese!" I shrieked again.

I felt his presence behind me, and the weight taken off my hands as it was placed down beside me.

"Are you ok?"

"I'm fine. I just lost my grip is all. Thank you." I replied, rubbing my hands together.

"Is that the last one?"

"Over here it is. How are you doing with the ones in the back?"

"I'm about to start loading them into the truck. You good to help or do you wanna take a break?"

"I'm good. We can take all the breaks we need when this shit is over and done with." He smiled at me. "What?"

"Nothing. I just like the way you think and work. Let's get this over with. All of these, including what is at home should last us through the winter and then some."

"I sure as shit hope so. I'm tired of these damn canisters." I joked and helped him bring them all out to the truck and load them up. Once everything was secured down, we were on our way back home to load everything back off just as the sun set.

"I'm going to find a place to park this thing. I'll be back."

"Wait. I'll put the emergency bags in there just in case we need it for later."

"Hurry up Babe. I'm fuckin beat."

"Don't rush me sir. I'm sore as hell and can't move that fast." I teased. Well, not really. My body really ached, and I couldn't wait to be done and over with this day. I made haste and returned rather quickly with the pre-packed bags from the basement. I hopped up in the truck.

"You're coming with me?"

"Why wouldn't I? Just start the truck and come on."

After dropping the truck off and taking another half hour walk back to the house, we were able to sit down for a minute and relax. The cabin was a mess and neither one of us had the energy to do anything about it. The candles flickered off in the distance, but the calming aroma filled the entire space. My hand was in his as he rubbed it gently and looked around the room very satisfied with today's work.

I finally mustered up the strength to get us some water and sat back in my chair and drank from it while he made us something to eat. My skin felt so clammy and overall, I felt disgusting and was wet from sweat so I decided to take a quick shower before the food was ready.

In and out as usual. There was no need to stay any longer in that cold ass water than was necessary. When I came out, he already had our food plated and we sat quietly and ate together peacefully in the soft glow of the lamp, the heaters and the candle. It couldn't have been a more relaxing moment.

He went and took his shower while I cleaned up in the kitchen after we ate and neither one of us wasted any time getting to sleep that night. Wrapped up in each other's arms as usual.

Keep It Up

My body ached and was sore as I sat up and stretched. Reese was still asleep as I completed my morning routine and stayed asleep for another hour or so after while I ate peacefully in my chair.

"How long you been up?"

I jumped a little from the sudden break of silence then rubbed my back from the pain. "About an hour."

Before he disappeared in the bathroom, he gave me a kiss. When he came back, he sat down beside me.

"I'm sore as hell too."

"Take your shirt off and go lay down."

"Damn. So bossy today." he joked but he did what I demanded as I grabbed the baby oil.

"You know you like it. Shut up."

"I do but keep it up and you're gonna get something back for that smart ass mouth."

"Hush and relax."

Baby oil was poured on his back as I sat on top of him giving him a long massage. Special attention was given to his shoulders and shoulder blades where he carried most of the weight and complained about. Just as he had massaged my back, I massaged him making sure to relieve all the tension.

When I was done, I hovered over him and stared at his beautiful, chocolate skin. My lips came close to his back and kissed it ever so softly which caused him to flinch. I couldn't help myself and kissed over his entire back.

"Keep it up and you're going to get more than a few kisses."

I slowed down but didn't stop and finally, he had had enough and rolled over to face me with low eyes. He sat up before his lips connected with mine passionately. My arms and legs wrapped around him pulling him in closer.

He flipped me over on my back and soon all his weight was on me as the passion and lust we had bottled up for each other was unleashed. Our hands wandered over each other's bodies in exploration and admiration for one another. Our tongues interlocked gracefully as we took each other's breath away.

Soon, his lips moved to my neck as his hands made their way down to my thighs where they were gripped firmly. As he hit my spot, I moaned softly. He knew where it was, and he was relentless on it, making me wetter with every tongue swirl and suck he gave to it.

My shirt was carelessly tossed to the side before he licked and sucked on my nipples. Each breast was firmly in his grasps and his attention alternated between the both of them then back to my neck where he gently bit down. I allowed it before I moved away. The feeling was too great for me to bear, and he smirked at my actions.

As my body writhed under him from the pleasure, I felt his erection growing steadily on my thigh which only made me want him more. He couldn't take it anymore and my underwear was pulled down and tossed to the side before he gazed at my now naked body before diving in.

His soft lips touched my wet pussy and I gasped from the unexpected feeling but welcomed it all the same. He licked up all my delectable juice as his tongue paid special attention to my throbbing clit.

The sensation seared down my spine to my toes as his tongue swirled around, filling me with erotic ecstasy. His hands were greedy, and he gripped my breasts firmly causing me to dig my nails deep into his back as bliss and satisfaction overtook me.

I could feel his warm breath on my thighs as he kissed them tenderly. His finger slowly entered my passion and stroked it slowly feeling every part of my inside fortress. My body tensed up and my heart fluttered in my chest as he ran his finger in and out moving deeper with every stroke.

The feeling was too great, and I tried to run from it, but his strong hand that was wrapped around my thigh wouldn't allow me to move. In fact, he brought me closer to his face. I had no choice but to take it and moaned loudly, trying to catch my breath in between. Complete control over my body was given to him and he took it with force. I loved every minute of it.

I could feel myself about to climax. He could feel it too and his tongue swirled faster around my clit. I tried to move away but there was nowhere to go. He held me firmly as he continued to please me. My body convulsed as I released into his mouth and on his finger. He didn't stop and the more he kept going, the more I tried to run away from the euphoria.

He finally stopped but only after he had sucked all the juice from my fruit. He looked up at me, sweat dripping from my face. Out of breath. Energy drained. But he wasn't done with me yet.

He kissed my lips again, then asked in a soft, quiet and sexy tone, "Are you ready?" I nodded my head and anxiously waited as he revealed his large erect missile.

As he gently entered, I bit his shoulder trying not to yell from the pressure, pain and pleasure he gave to my tight pussy. My nails, once again, dug into his back but he didn't complain as he slowly, lovingly and passionately stroked.

I held my breath as he stroked deeper and longer. My legs wrapped around his waist allowing him to go even deeper. "Don't hold it in." he said, in a low, sexy voice. "Let that shit out." I moaned softly. "Yea, let that shit out." The tone of his voice drove me crazy making me wetter for his enjoyment.

As I came once again on him, he paused for a moment to feel me throb on his dick before he continued stroking. Each stroke a little faster. A little deeper. Each stroke made me whine a little louder.

"I'm about to cum." he said, and with three more thrusts he pulled out. His warm juice squirted out on my stomach before he collapsed on top of me. I held him tight with my arms and legs and didn't want to let go. Our breathing was erratic, and our hearts raced fiercely.

We laid there for quite some time trying to catch our breath and regain the lost energy. He looked up at me with a smile on his face and I had no choice but to smile back at him before kissing his forehead gently. This kiss only caused him to want me more as he kissed my lips. Once again, the lust between us began to ignite.

Reluctantly, I pushed him back as my heart rate began to increase and my stomach fluttered. "Don't start me up again."

He licked and bit down on my neck before getting up. "I won't. Not yet anyway."

His naked chocolate body disappeared into the bathroom before he came out to clean his mess that was on me. He disappeared once again and I sat on the edge of the bed trying to compose myself.

Deep breaths were taken before I finally stood to my feet and made my way to the bathroom. My legs felt so weak. My body felt amazing. After cleaning up, I joined him in the bed where his arms wrapped tightly around me. My head nestled comfortably on his chest. My face... a big smile spread across it before exhaustion got the best of me from the glorious activities that took place moments before.

It was midday now and the sun was high in the sky when I realized I was still naked. Quickly, I covered myself up and tried to find a new set of clothes before Maureese realized what I was doing, but it was too late.

"Why are you trying to cover yourself up? I done seen every spectacular part of your body already."

My face flushed as I turned my head to look at him. He had a huge smile on his face as he sat up to get a better view. "Stop looking at me." I said shyly.

His smile didn't falter as he simply asked, "Why?"

I quickly put on my shirt, hoodie and sweatpants and walked over to him, feeling so much better now that I was clothed. "Cuz, I feel weird when you stare at me like that."

"That's not what you were saying a few hours ago." he chuckled.

I sucked my teeth and walked over to the kitchen. His heavy footsteps followed me and before I knew it, his warm embrace was around me.

His package bulged against my ass. I reached around to touch him and realized he was still naked as well. I felt myself blush once again.

He turned me around and gazed into my eyes. His glance was so soft and loving. I shied away and looked down. I quickly looked back up once I realized I was staring right at his dick. I blushed even harder. My reactions seemed to have amused him because he made his dick jump causing my focus to be drawn back to it.

I grabbed it in my hands and played with it leisurely before letting it go. I felt so shy. I don't even know why. Sensing my shyness, he walked away and put his clothes on. He was still smiling ear to ear as he did so.

That whole interaction caused me to lose my train of thought as I thought to myself, "Why am I in the kitchen?" It came back to me, and I grabbed a bottle of water and went to drink it in the chair. I was soon joined by a fully dressed Maureese who sat in his chair beside me.

He grabbed my hand and pulled it to his lips. He kissed it ever so gently and it brought back the pleasure he had given me earlier today. I pulled my hand back and shied away once again. He was definitely teasing me.

I shifted uncomfortably in my seat as I tried to drink my water. I tried to do it in a slight way, but he noticed. "You ok?" he asked, grabbing my hand. Differently this time.

"It hurts a little bit." I admitted.

"I'm sorry, I didn't mean to hurt you. I can get carried away sometimes…"

"It's just been a while and… you're not a small dude if you know what I mean."

Another smile fell upon his face as I stroked his ego a bit. "I know what you mean. My apologies."

"Pshh, don't apologize. It was amazing!" I blushed again and shifted about in my chair.

"Why don't you go lay back down then Babe. Relax yourself." He stood to his feet and gently helped me up to mine. After he laid me down, he pulled the covers over me. "Get some rest. You might need it for later." he hinted.

A smile splashed across my face as I shook my head. "I wish we could watch tv or something. I miss my nature shows." I blurted out of nowhere and pure boredom.

"Look around, we are surrounded by nature. This is the nature show." he amused.

"You know damn well what I meant."

He chuckled. "I know."

Silence fell about in the cabin once again as we were both in our own little worlds for the time being. I couldn't get my mind off of how amazing this man made me feel. It was almost too unreal. The feeling he gave me almost made me forget about all the other bullshit that was going on around us. The thought kept popping up in my head of how complete I felt now. Like some hopeless romantic type shit.

I couldn't help the feelings I had towards him. It still frightened me at how soon these feelings appeared but thinking back on all that we had been through... we were with each other nonstop, every day for over a week. Depending on each other for survival.

My growling stomach forced me up and into the kitchen. His eyes followed me from his chair that he sat in before he spoke. "What are you doing? Go back and lay down."

"I'm hungry. I want to eat something."

"Go lay down, I'll fix you something." He demanded. His voice was stern

"Reese, I'm not immobile. I can fix something myself." I argued back.

"I'm not saying that you are. I feel bad I made you feel this way. Let me take care of you."

With those words, I couldn't argue back. The cabinet door closed, and I did as he requested and laid back down in the bed.

"What do you want to eat?"

"Surprise me."

It didn't take long before it was done, and he brought my food over to me. I sat up slowly and looked at what he prepared. It actually looked good. Like he cooked, cooked the meal from scratch.

I waited for him to hand me the plate, but he didn't. Instead, he fed me bite by bite until I was finished. I thought it was the sweetest thing ever. Afterwards, he took my plate into the kitchen and ate his dinner in his chair that he brought over next to me.

"That was so good! Thanks Babe." I said to him as he was eating his food.

"I'm glad you like it my Luv." He took another big bite from his spoon.

I could never get over how fast he ate. He was done in no time, washed the dishes and was back by my side. "How are you feeling?" he asked as he sat down in his chair. He leaned his face close to mine.

"Much better. Thank you. How are you feeling?" I said returning the gesture and leaning into his personal space.

"I'm fucking great!" he said, in a perky tone that caused me to burst out laughing. He laughed with me too. "Nah, but for real. I'm doing great." A smile spread over his face. "Never better."

"Well, I'm glad to hear that." My nose touched his as I gave him an Eskimo kiss. "I need to go take a shower now. I smell like hot sex." I teased slowly standing to my feet.

"You got it? You need some help? Maybe you know... Undressing?"

I turned around in a humorous shock. "Really? No. I'm good, I got it thanks." He laughed as I proceeded into the bathroom.

After my brief shower I realized I had forgotten to grab clean clothes. The towel was wrapped tightly around me as I made my way to the main cabin area. Although he said, not one word, his eyes never left me as I tried to find something clean to wear.

Obviously, just looking was not enough for this man and soon, I felt his presence behind me. Then, my towel "accidentally" fell, exposing my naked body to him.

He growled slightly before picking me up and gently placing me on my back in the bed. As his hands explored every inch of my body, I couldn't help but to get turned on again. I paused and stared into his eyes before kissing his lips gently, letting him know I was ready for more of what he desperately wanted to give me.

His clothes were tossed to the side with my help and his body was pressed tightly on mine once again. The lust rushed back and turned to passion as we caressed and explored each other's body with... Not just our hands. Before I knew it, he was back inside my wet, tight temple filling me with pleasure all over again.

"I'm not hurting you, am I?" he asked in between kissing.

"No. Not at all. Go deeper." I yelled and he obeyed, sending me over the top. I couldn't control myself as he stroked deeper and deeper at my requests. Each stroke once again made me wetter and wetter. He drove me crazy with how he pleasured my body. He knew the right places to touch at the right time to set me off.

I came at least three times before he finally came on my stomach again. He looked me deep in my eyes before he kissed me, which only turned me on even more. I was greedy and wanted more.

He went into the bathroom and cleaned himself up before returning with a washcloth to clean me up. After he did, I gripped him up and began the passion all over again.

When we were done, the sun was coming up and we had collapsed on the bed. Drained of all energy. Even more than the first time.

He laid on top of me. Our limbs intertwined as we tried to catch our sanity back. It took a long while before he rolled over next to me and finally passed out. His steady breathing was my melody for sleep.

Nice to Meet You

Three days had passed since we last stepped foot out of the cabin. Most of our nights and days were full of lust and recuperation. Nothing else seemed to matter. In that time, our bond had grown strong. We had a better sense of one on another and it brought us to a whole new level of companionship.

I looked around at the cabin that was a total mess. Clothes, clean and dirty, were everywhere. Just thrown about and the bed was a total mess. What was the point of getting dressed anyway? I rolled over and began to kiss Reese once again. In his half sleep state, he kissed me back with a smile on his face.

"Good morning to you too my Luv."

"Good morning." I said in a cheerful voice. "I'm going to get breakfast started." I said as I slowly began to get up. My body ached, but it was worth the pain. Oh, so worth it.

One of his shirts was thrown over my head after I completed my morning routine. He watched from the comfort of the bed as I made our breakfast and brought it over to where he was. He half expected me to hand him his plate, but instead, I fed him slowly. I think he enjoyed the special attention.

"I wish I could cook you a real meal and not this canned food shit."

He chuckled. "Maybe one day you will. It was still good."

"I'm glad you enjoyed it."

As I cleaned the kitchen, I heard his footsteps come up behind me. His large hands cupped both of my cheeks before he disappeared into the bathroom. Now that the kitchen was cleaned, I moved to the main cabin area before he reappeared again.

"Damn Baby, you drained me." he said, stretching his entire body.

My eyes wandered down his half naked body and I bit my lip before responding. "You keep walking around like that, you may have to tap out." He covered his chest, and I couldn't help but to laugh.

"Give me a minute and I'll help you clean up some." He sat down on the bed to compose himself and fully wake up.

"Don't worry about it. I got it. Relax."

Completely ignoring my request, he fully got dressed and started helping out anyway. Shit, I wasn't going to complain.

The cabin was fully organized in an hour, and we sat down in the chairs and admired our work. "That dirty clothes pile is stacking up. We gotta do something about it."

"What do you mean we have to do SOMETHING about it?" I laughed. "We have to wash clothes."

"Don't get smart with me, woman. You know what I meant." he joked.

I glanced over lazily at the pile and commented. "I'm not doing that shit today."

"I'm not saying today. I'm just saying in general." He paused for a moment. "I was actually thinking we should go for target practice today."

My ears perked up. "That sounds... interesting."

"It's about time you learned how to shoot and get comfortable with a gun." He stood up and walked over to the gun bag and brought it over to his chair. He pulled out a few and gently placed them in his lap. "You liked this one right?" He held up the one that I had a while back.

I took it timidly in my hand and examined it. "Yea, that's the one."

"Be careful, it's loaded." he said,, and I gently and quickly placed it on the floor beside us. He laughed. "Don't be scared of it. See, that's why we are going to practice with it. You gotta be comfortable with it and learn how to use it properly."

"I kind of figured that's what the target practice was for." I remarked.

He stopped doing what he was doing and stared at me for a bit. I shrugged my shoulders and he mumbled, "Smart ass."

"I heard that." I retorted.

"You were supposed to." he remarked back. I laughed to myself. "Come on. Get dressed, I'm ready to go!" So much enthusiasm was in his voice. I couldn't help but to jump into action and do as he commanded.

We both got dressed, packed our weapons and emergency bags, put on our boots before heading out the door. It was surprisingly beautiful outside. Especially since we had been cooped up in the house for three days straight.

I followed his lead as we walked down the path we had marked a few days before. We wanted to go out far so as to not draw too much attention to where we laid our heads.

After about an hour's walk, he stopped and put down the bags. I did the same and walked up beside him as he looked around for a good target to shoot at. "There." he said, pointing off in the short distance. "You see that tree with the knot on it? That's our target."

He dug around in the bag and handed me my gun of which I took timidly and examined it. "I'm not ready for this Reese."

"You better get ready. Want me to go first?" I nodded my head. "Fine. Pay attention."

He stepped ahead of me, and I watched attentively. The way he held the gun up. The way he pointed it as he aimed. The way he took a breath before he pulled the trigger. The shot rang out loudly, startling me and I jumped. I thought my heart stopped. He shot another shot. Then another and another back-to-back.

As the bullets hit the tree, pieces of bark flew off into shreds. I think he only missed his target once. He looked at me and saw the expression on my face. He grinned.

"You good?"

"Yea. It was just louder than I had expected. Nice shooting."

"Thanks. You ready now?"

"I think so."

I composed myself as I walked up to where he was. He stood behind me and helped me hold the gun up and how to hold my hands. He took a few steps back leaving me on my own. My heart raced. My hands began to sweat. I aimed the gun at the target. Took a deep breath and exhaled slowly. I pulled the trigger, and nothing happened. Confused, I looked at the gun.

"Take the safety off Babe." he laughed. I cut my eyes over at him before doing what he said,.

I re-focused, took another deep breath and exhaled slowly again. I pulled the trigger again and the gun jumped back as it fired. I missed. I felt a little defeated but tried again.

"Hold your wrists steady next time." he yelled. I took his words into consideration.

I pointed, aimed and focused on the target and pulled the trigger. Once, twice, and three times. Each time I missed, but my adrenaline began to course through my veins. My focus became clearer and narrowed. I repositioned my weight into something more comfortable for me, took a breath and pulled the trigger. I saw the bark fly from the tree. I hit the target.

I turned back at Reese as my face beamed. He was smiling ear to ear for me. "Nice job Babe!" he clapped. I focused again and pulled the trigger a few more times. Each time, the bark splintered off the tree.

He walked up beside me when I lowered the gun. I was more than ecstatic. "I think you're a natural." he said,.

"You think so?"

"Hell yea."

I looked down at the big ass shotgun he held in his hands. "You're going to shoot that?"

"That's what I brought it out here for. It's been a minute since I shot one. I have to get used to it." He looked at me looking at it. "You want to try this one too?"

"I'll let you handle that one boss."

"Ok Miss."

He stood in position and aimed at the target with the shotgun. When the trigger was pulled, the gun roared. The knot on the tree vanished leaving a hole where it had once been.

I stood in total stupefaction. "Holy shit!"

"Yea boy!" His voice was filled with satisfaction. "That's what the fuck I'm talking about." He raised the gun again and fired it. The hole in the tree widened as he hit his mark. More bark splintered off. He turned back to me. "You sure you don't want to try?"

I thought for a minute. "I'm going to stick to this one for now."

He went over to the bag and pulled out another handgun. "Here, try this one out."

I looked at it. "What's the difference? I like this one."

"You have to practice with them all."

I grabbed the gun from his hand and stepped forward. "I have no target. You blew it away." I laughed.

"Just shoot."

I turned around and aimed the gun. I made sure the safety was off first this time before I took a breath and fired. I missed. I repositioned myself and shot again. More bark came off the poor tree.

"Can you feel a difference between the two?"

"Yea. This one feels heavier. I kind of like it."

"See."

"But… I still want mine." I reassured.

"Just don't forget to practice with them all. Ok?"

"Ok." I whined.

We took turns firing the guns. Each time, I got better. I was able to aim faster and not have to take my long, exaggerated breath before I fired. I was able to focus and aim at the target much more easily and not have to slow down and think before shooting. I think he was right. I was a natural and I found a new addiction.

"Ready to head back? It's starting to get dark." I said as I looked up at the sky. The sun was fading fast behind the trees.

"Yea, let's start heading back."

We cleaned up our area and packed away the guns we had out. Reese put one in his holster as he always did and when we were done, we began heading back to the cabin.

The sun had melted into the dark background. The sky was a beautiful indigo blue and there was no moon out. The dark swiftly engulfed us making the markings on the trees barely visible. Along with the dark, came the frigid autumn air.

I moved closer to him and intertwined my arm with his. He embraced my grip and rubbed my hand soothingly. "I think we're almost there." he whispered to me.

Before I could respond back, we heard a noise off in the distance. The both of us stopped dead in our tracks and listened intently to our surroundings. We heard the noise again. Rustling leaves. The sound was coming right at us.

We silently moved off the path and ducked behind the overgrown brush. A tree was at our backs, and I could feel Reese pull his gun off his hip.

The crunching leaves got closer until they were a few feet away. "Is anyone out there?" the man's voice sprang out of the darkness. My eyes grew big, and my heart raced. I felt Maureese's hands cover my mouth signifying to stay quiet.

"Hello?" the voice wearily rang out again. As he called, his footsteps fumbled and were coming straight in our direction. "Please! I'm hurt. I need help." the male voice said.

I didn't know what to do. I wanted to help, but at the same time, he could have been lying about his situation. He could hurt us or worse. Or, he could seriously be injured and really need our help. He could also become an asset to us giving us an extra hand. He could also become a liability and be another mouth to feed.

Maureese tapped my shoulder signaling to stay put as he stood up. I grabbed his hand, but he shook me off and held my shoulder still before leaving my side.

"Please help me." The man's voice continued pleading. His footsteps were staggered. I could tell he was not ok.

I heard the familiar heavy footsteps walk away from me as the leaves crunched under his boots. I could only make out a faint image of him in the darkness. He was holding his gun up and aiming it directly at the man's chest as he slowly and cautiously walked in his direction.

"Who's there?" the man's voice yelled out. "Please don't hurt me. I mean no harm." He stopped walking.

"Who are you?" Maureese's voice bellowed out sternly. His footsteps increased as he got closer to the man.

"My name is… is Tyshawn." the man stuttered. Next thing I heard was a loud yell from him and a scuffle on the ground. I was ready to go into action until the man yelled after a few seconds. "Please, let me go. I don't mean you any harm man."

"You have any weapons on you?" Maureese asked. I could hear him patting the man down.

"No, nothing, just my cell phone."

"Is it on?" Reese asked with much concern in his voice.

"No. No. It died. You wouldn't happen to have a charger on you, would you? I need to call my family to find out if they are ok. My sister. I need to know if she's ok."

"No, I don't have a charger. Don't ever use that phone."

"What? Why not?"

Was he serious right now?

"It attracts those things." Reese said in a modest way.

"Oh gees, the crawlers?"

"That's what you call them?"

"Yea man." The man paused. His voice got soft. "They killed my girl and my son. I just need to know if my little sister is ok." Maureese didn't say a word. "Can I get up now? Can you stop pointing that thing at me? I don't mean any harm man. The last thing I want is a bullet in my chest." he rambled on with an extreme country accent.

I heard Maureese lower his gun, but he didn't put it away. His footsteps came my way and my heart raced as he grabbed my arm and pulled me up to my feet. My legs throbbed as I stood up from the lack of circulation due to how I was crouching.

"Where'd you go?" Tyshawn yelled from the darkness.

"I'm here." Reese retorted back to him. He pulled me alongside him and put his finger to mouth as if to tell me to stay quiet. My footsteps rustled unwantedly in the dry fall leaves.

"Who else is there?" Tyshawn asked. Fear stuck in his voice.

"My partner in crime." Reese simply said back to him. "Come on." he continued as we began walking back to the cabin.

We got back home in less than ten minutes. Reese unlocked and opened the door keeping me by his side as we all entered. The faint light of the lamp came on burning my eyes as they adjusted to the light.

I looked over at our newcomer who already had his eyes on me. He was covered in blood. Old and new blood. The rancid and familiar smell of death filled my nostrils bringing back bad memories. His shirt was basically shreds and he had three claw marks on his chest.

Tyshawn said nothing. Only stared at me until he finally broke his silence. "Who is this beautiful lady?"

His words didn't sit too well with Reese nor me. I could tell by Reese's tone that he was trying to be polite as Tyshawn still examined me. "Are you thirsty? Or hungry?" Reese asked. His voice was stern and aggravated by the actions of the newcomer. He stood between the two of us.

"Both if you don't mind." Tyshawn said politely.

Maureese went, unwillingly into the kitchen and grabbed a water bottle and some food. As he did so, Tyshawn made his way over to me. I backed up slowly until my back hit the wall. An uneasy and uncomfortable feeling fell upon me by his actions.

He held out his hand. "Very nice to meet you." he said, with a stark grin across his face. "What's your name?"

I hesitantly placed my hand in his and replied, "Natalie." I tried to pull my hand away but held on to it and brought it to his lips to kiss it.

"It's a pleasure to meet you, Natalie." he said, with a smile.

Reese came out of the kitchen area and shoved the food and water into Tyshawn's chest and pushed him hard to the other side of the room and held him up against the wall. He didn't say anything as he got in Tyshawn's face. Reese's facial expressions explained it all. It was full of anger and very threatening. It even scared me. No words needed to be spoken.

Tyshawn threw his hands up in submission and Reese backed away. "After you finish eating, we will attend to your wounds." he said, in a hostile tone. After he spoke, he walked over to where I was and posted up on the wall beside me. His jaw was clenched. I looked down and saw that he still had his gun on his hip.

Tyshawn guzzled down his food and water. Even faster than I had seen Reese do. "Thank you so much. May I have more?"

"We don't have any more to spare."

"There's more pears in the cabinet... If you'd like..." Reese and I spoke at the same time. I looked up at him who looked frustratingly down at me before walking into the kitchen once again and grabbing the pears from the cabinet. He walked over and handed him the pears and returned to my side.

"Thank you so much." Tyshawn said as he devoured those just as he did the first go round.

I walked past Reese and dug around in the bags and pulled out a fresh shirt, hoodie and sweatpants for Tyshawn and handed them to him. Maureese didn't say a word as he watched my actions and kept looking at Tyshawn and studying him.

"There's a shower down there if you would like to freshen up. There's no hot water, but it's better than nothing." My back pressed up against the wall next to Reese as I spoke.

"Thank you so much." he said, and disappeared into the bathroom.

I let out a slight sigh of relief. Maureese scratched his head and sat on the bed. He had this… look splashed on his face.

"What's wrong Reese?" I whispered sitting next to him on the bed.

"I don't know about this guy man. I'm not feeling the way he's looking at you. I'm not feeling it at all." His jaw was still tense and locked.

I nodded my head in agreement. I was in the same boat as him.

"I mean, what if it's not just him?" What if there are others with him? What if he's with a group or some shit? Now he knows where we stay and can lead them right to us." He buried his face in his hands and I rubbed his back for comfort. "I just…" he continued and paused before speaking again. He looked me dead in the eyes. "I just don't want anything to happen to you."

"Nothing is going to happen to me." I rested my head on his shoulder. "Nothing is going to happen to US."

"You saw how he was looking at you Babe?" he continued.

There was a brief pause before I spoke. "But he didn't do anything. And I think you put him in his place. He's not stupid."

"Not good enough..." he began but was interrupted by Tyshawn's entrance into the main cabin area.

He had on his sweatpants, but no shirt. We could see the scratch marks on his chest and there was no way they were human or from an animal. We stood up and walked towards him. "What the hell did this?" I asked examining the scratches a bit closely. "Reese, can you go get the first aid kit?"

He left my side briefly and came back with what I asked for before Tyshawn spoke about his wounds. "It was the crawlers." he simply said.

I instructed him to sit down on the floor as I prepared everything to clean him up. "THEY did THAT to you?" Reese asked following Tyshawn and I into the middle of the room. "Where was this at?" he asked.

"Down on the Westside."

There was a brief pause again. "Wait, are you from around there?"

"Yea. I grew up over there."

"Wait, you know Manny?" Reese asked with a different tone in his voice.

"Yea, Manny's my cousin."

"Oh shit. You're Ty Ty?"

"Yea, yea, that's me."

"Oh shit, what's good bro? I thought you looked familiar. Kinda hard to tell with all that shit on ya face. What's good?"

I rolled my eyes as they continued to talk about their childhood and reminisce about things growing up. I interrupted for a moment when I was ready to clean his wound.

"This is gonna sting a little bit." I said and poured peroxide on the wound.

"Ahh shit yo." Tyshawn yelped.

"Ahh, stop bein a bitch." Reese said. He was much more relaxed now and his country accent was coming through. I was just relieved that there wasn't going to be any bullshit tonight.

I poured the peroxide on the wound at least three more times and each time I found that it bubbled up just as much as the first time, which I found quite strange. I wrapped it up with gauze and tape and stood up off the floor. They were STILL talking.

"You done Babe?" Reese asked me as I began to walk to the kitchen to wash my hands.

"Babe?" Tyshawn interrupted. "That's all you big boy?"

"Yea man. That's my girl right there." I felt myself blush a bit as I washed my hands. A kiss was placed on my neck, followed by a big ass hug from behind. I turned around and smiled sharply at Reese as he continued to brag. "That's my baby right there." He rubbed my face gently before walking back to Tyshawn.

I grabbed myself something quick to eat from the cabinet and walked over to the bed. It was the only place I could really sit. Reese was in my chair, talking to Tyshawn who was sitting in his chair. I sat quietly as the two of them talked and caught up on family and stories they heard about people from their old block.

"Yo, man, where are you staying at?" I heard Reese ask.

"Everywhere and nowhere. After this shit hit, I've just been wandering around trying to stay out of trouble. You mind if I crash here tonight?"

"Yea, yea, no problem. We'll set something up for you to sleep on."

I got up and grabbed a few extra blankets and pillows from our stash and spread them neatly in the opposite corner of our bed. "Thanks Babe." Reese said, giving me a hug and a kiss before I went and sat back down on the bed.

"Aye, thanks man. I really appreciate it." Ty said. "Before I lay down, you mind if I go to the bathroom right quick?"

"Absolutely. You know where it is."

Reese sat down beside me on the bed. "How crazy is this? I run into my people out here?"

I smirked. "It is very crazy. Glad you ran into someone you know."

"Yea, man, we go way back. Manny was like a brother to me. We always used to chill with this dude." I didn't say a word. I just smiled. "What's wrong?" he asked gently grabbing my face.

"Nothing Babe, I'm just tired is all."

"Come. Lay down then."

"I have to change my clothes. We've been outside all day with these on." I replied.

"Ok. Go change when he comes out then." He grabbed my face and gave me an Eskimo kiss before giving me a real kiss on my lips.

Tyshawn came out of the bathroom as soon as I finished grabbing my night clothes. The bathroom door closed behind me. Fully this time as I put my night clothes on and, while I hated wearing pants to sleep in, I had to this time.

Back in the main cabin, the lights were dimmed for me already and the men were still talking. I honestly didn't know he could talk that much. I laughed to myself.

Luckily, my spot in the bed was closest to the wall and I laid with my back towards them and tried to go to sleep. I was so uncomfortable in the pants, plus, this was NOT my usual sleeping position AND my sleeping music was chatting it up with an old friend. His voice still soothed me, and soon I was fast asleep.

Good Dreams Can Come True Too

The next morning, I woke up to find a cold spot next to me in the bed. The cabin was eerily quiet as I scanned around for Reese, but there was no sign of either of them. My eyes glanced over to the door and saw that his boots were missing along with the tattered shoes Tyshawn had on. The door was locked, and as I glanced around the cabin, I spotted a letter laying in my chair. I quickly got up to read it.

Babe,

We went to the plaza so he could get some clothes. I didn't want to wake you. Be back soon.

I let out a sigh of relief before walking into the kitchen to grab something to eat. The heater came on and I stood by it for a while trying to warm myself up as I ate my fruit.

My eyes glanced over at the dirty clothes pile that was stacked up and I sighed again figuring I might as well get the shit started. At least it would distract my mind a bit while he was gone. Once my fruit was done, I walked over to the pile of clothes and sorted through them before making a clothes washing station to help with the process. Water and detergent was added to the machine as well as a few dirty clothes and I began washing. The heater had to go after some time due to the physical movements of washing.

Load after load after load, I cleaned, rinsed and spun dried. I missed a washing machine. I'm not gonna lie. Back then, I thought it was a chore to have to lug all my clothes to the laundromat. I'll take that over this any day. It's amazing how things you once took for granted can be something you wish for the most.

It took me hours to wash all of the clothes we had, but it was finally done, and they were hung up around the cabin to air dry. The fresh smell of detergent and fabric softener filled the space.

I sat down in my chair and wondered where they were. What was taking them so long? I looked outside and saw the sun was beginning to set and I started to worry. Just as my worry set in, I heard two voices off in the distance, then two figures appeared walking towards the cabin. My heart fluttered and I got butterflies as I heard the sound of Maureese's voice.

I went to put something more suitable on and opened the cabin door just as Reese was coming up the steps. I flung my arms around him, and he dropped his bags he was carrying and embraced my hug.

"Hey Babe!" he said, kissing my forehead.

I hit him hard in his chest and spoke in a baby voice, "What took you so long?"

He grabbed where I punched in pain and shock and smiled. "I'm sorry, we got caught up talking. Guy talk." He grabbed the bags that were on the ground, and I helped to bring them inside. Tyshawn followed in after him and he gave me a weird, pervy look and licked his lips. I looked at him weird and stepped back away from him.

Reese's words broke my train of thought. "You washed clothes? I didn't want you to wash them all by yourself. You could have left me something to wash."

"What else was I going to do to pass the time? It's cool. Everything is done, we just have to wait and let them dry. You can fold them and put them away, how about that?"

"What? That's a woman's job." Tyshawn interrupted. "Laundry is a woman's job."

"That's not how we work around here." Reese replied back sternly. "That's not how we work at all." He gave me a kiss on the lips before taking off his boots and going through the bags he had just brought back.

Tyshawn did the same and they both unpacked one item at a time until all the bags were empty.

I glanced over everything they had brought back. It was mainly clothes. Some food items neither of us liked. A few more knives, kitchen utensils, male personal care items, things along those lines.

"I got you a few things too Babe." Reese said holding up some items of clothing. "It's nothing special though."

I smiled and took the items from his hands. "Thank you!"

"Hey, you think you could make us something to eat while I put all this stuff away?" Reese asked.

"Of course." was my response as I headed into the kitchen. As I was working, I heard Reese's heavy footsteps come towards me. I smiled at his presence, but I didn't stop working until a cold, metal item was placed around my neck.

I looked down to see what it was, and it was a beautiful gold sun pendant necklace with tribal signs in the sun flares. I turned around and looked at him who was smiling ear to ear waiting for my response. I wrapped my arms around his neck, giving him a big hug before I spoke. "Thank you, thank you, thank you! I love it." So much excitement was in my voice as I admired the necklace.

"I'm glad you like it." he said,. His smile still splashed upon his face. "There's more over here."

"Really?!" I said looking to where he was pointing at. It was a huge pile of jewelry laid out on the bed. I walked over to it and skimmed it all with my eyes. "Let me finish making your food, and I'll go through it!" I walked back over to the kitchen and finished preparing the food. But not before I caught a glimpse of Tyshawn's grimace on his face.

I didn't think too much about it. Figured he was feeling some type away because he was missing his girlfriend and son. Yet here we were exchanging presents and being luvy duvy in front of his face. My smile fell a little thinking about what he must be going through.

I finished with the food and handed each of them their plate. They were both sitting in a chair, and I noticed there were three chairs now. I grabbed my plate and sat next to Reese, and we began to eat.

Tyshawn simply looked at the food in disgust. I broke the awkward ass silence. "Did you guys run into any problems while you were out there?" I asked before taking a bite.

"Nah. No problems Babe. I'm glad there weren't any…"

"This shit is cold man." Tyshawn interrupted. "What kind of woman you have, to serve us cold ass food?"

I looked up at Reese whose jaw was locked. He looked frustrated and aggravated. "What the hell do you suppose she cook it on Ty?"

"The stove or the heater. Something."

"And then you'd be complaining about how I was taking too long to fix the food." I blurted. "How about you shut the fuck up and be thankful that you actually have food to eat." I continued to rant.

Reese looked over at me in shock, surprised at my outburst. But what I said was true, so he didn't say a word. Until…

"How about you shut the fuck up and get in a woman's place." Tyshawn yelled back.

"Whoa, whoa, whoa. You not gonna talk to my girl like that bruh." Reese intervened and sat up in his chair.

"Your girl needs to check her attitude when speaking to a man."

"My girl is just fine. YOU need to check your attitude when speaking to HER. I told you before bro, we do shit differently over here. Ain't no 'man's job' or 'woman's job'. We do shit here equally."

"And that's the problem. That's why you get cold ass food and a stank ass attitude from this bitch." He threw his plate on the floor.

Reese put his food down quickly and stood up out of his seat. He angrily walked in front of Tyshawn who also stood up. They were staring each other in the face. "Watch what you say to her bro. Don't call her no bitch." Reese said in a low, threatening tone. His hands bald up into fists. "You wanna stay here? You respect her or you can go."

"I'm just saying, you deserve better than that ol' boy." Tyshawn backed down and backed away from Reese.

"She is better." Reese added as he sat back down in his chair. He picked up his plate and continued eating.

Tyshawn stormed out of the room and into the bathroom slamming the door behind him. Reese was furious. I touched his hand, and he didn't flinch. I stood up from my chair and put my plate in the kitchen before cleaning the mess up from Tyshawn.

"Don't pick that up Baby. I'll get it." he said, standing up. He put his plate in the kitchen and began to pick up Tyshawn's.

My eyes began to brim with tears, and I walked over to the bed and sat down. My face was buried in my hands and the tears streamed down. My throat was tight as I tried to hold them back. I felt Reese sit down next to me as he rubbed my back gently.

"What's wrong Babe? Don't cry." His voice was soft and gentle. "Don't let his words get to you."

"It just reminds me of how someone else used to talk to me is all." I wiped the tears from my cheeks before he took my face into his hands.

"He won't talk to you like that again, I promise." He wrapped me up in his arms as my tears soaked his shirt. "You know I'm here to listen whenever you're ready to talk."

I nodded my head under his embrace and pulled away before he walked over to the bathroom and knocked on the door assertively.

"Ty." His voice bellowed and I heard the bathroom door open. They began to talk quietly amongst themselves. I couldn't make out the words, so I just sat there in my sorrows.

A few minutes later, they both came from around the corner. Tyshawn stood in front of me and I blankly looked up at him. "I'm sorry man." he said, in a mellow tone. "I'm just not used to the way yall do things. With me and my girl, it was so much different. Even the way I saw my mom and pops do things was different than yall. I gotta respect it. You forgive me?"

He held out his hand. I really didn't want to hear shit he had to say, nor accept his lame ass excuse of an apology. I looked over at Reese who was standing there with hopeful eyes. I reluctantly took his hand and shook it without saying a word.

"Cool, cool." he said, as he went over to the chair and sat down in it.

My night clothes were grabbed before I went into the bathroom and closed and locked the door. Something I could never get used to doing. I took my brief cold shower, brushed my teeth and got dressed before slowly walking into the main cabin area. Reese was sitting in his chair next to Tyshawn, but they weren't speaking to one another.

I set my clothes down in the dirty clothes pile and went over to the bed and began sorting through all the jewelry that was brought back. I examined them closely. They appeared to be real gold, silver and diamonds. I turned and looked back at him, who had his eyes on me.

I held up a bracelet for him to see before I spoke. "Are these real?" I asked in a calm, timid voice.

He nodded his head. "They're real."

I lowered the bracelet back down. "Where did you get these?"

He stood up and walked over to me and sat down with the jewelry between us. "There was a pawn shop in one of the plazas we went to. The front of the store was fucked up, but the back of the store was untouched. I thought you might like some of these, so I grabbed them." He ran his hands over the jewelry and found a piece for himself. "I grabbed a few things for myself. So did he."

He put the solid gold, braided chain around his neck and pulled out two matching bracelets that I helped him put on. I sorted through the jewelry some more until I found matching bracelets to my necklace that was already around my neck. He helped me put them on and I stared at them in amazement. The gold and diamonds sparkled under the lamp light.

Never in my life had I ever had anything like this. Real jewelry? Real diamonds, gold and silver? That was just a dream that I had. But as I looked down at the jewels on my wrists, then back at the man that had brought them to me, I realized that some good dreams could come true too.

Tyshawn moved about in his chair until he finally stood to his feet. "I'm gonna go wash up bro." he said, in a solemn tone. His head hung low as he proceeded into the bathroom, closing the door behind him.

I stood up and stretched. Reese stood up with me and picked me up in his arms with a hug. He put me down and we stood there for a while, both admiring each other. His manly hand caressed my soft skin gently as I played in his beard a bit before he began kissing my lips. His kiss never stopped taking my breath away. Each time they touched mine, it was like the first.

I pulled away from him and took a few steps back. He looked at me confused. "You're turning me on." I said in a shy manner.

"I'm getting turned on too." He walked up to me again and gave me one final kiss before going to sit in his chair.

Tyshawn came out of the bathroom and sank down quietly in his chair. It seemed as though his morale was very low.

Reese got up and grabbed some clean clothes and walked over to where I sat on the bed. He pulled my face up so I could look up at him. "I'll be right back." he said, softly and disappeared into the bathroom.

I looked at the back of Tyshawn's head but said not one word to him. There was nothing to say to him honestly. I really just wanted him to leave. Wish he had never come here. He was going to be a problem and that was the last thing Reese and I needed.

I began to neatly put the jewelry back into the bag when he walked over to where I was. "You need help?" he asked with a low voice.

I looked up at him and shook my head. "No, I'm alright thanks." I responded. I hoped that he would just go away, but of course, he didn't.

I looked down at the task before me and I felt his hand touch my hair. I stopped and moved my head away. I looked up and asked in a stern tone. "What are you doing?"

"Nothing, I'm sorry. It's just that…" he paused for a minute and stared at me. "You're so beautiful."

I looked at him like he was fucking crazy. Did this guy have split personalities or something? Was he fucking insane?

"Yea, Reese thinks so as well." I snapped back.

He took a deep, aggravated breath before he returned to his seat. The bathroom door opened, and familiar footsteps walked into the main cabin room.

Reese put his clothes in the dirty clothes pile and looked at me. I glanced back up at him with a meek look on my face, then looked back down at what I was doing. "What's wrong Nat?"

I thought about telling him what happened, but I didn't want to hear any more yelling and arguing. I had had enough for the day. "Nothing Babe. I'm just tired is all."

He came over to my side and helped me finish putting everything away. "Come. Lay down then." he said, motioning for me to lay in the bed. The covers were pulled up over me as I laid in a fetal position staring at the wall. Gentle, soft strokes were given to my back before Reese went to sit in the chair next to Tyshawn.

I rolled my eyes and pulled the covers over my head. I was so frustrated. Usually, he would come and lay down next to me. He would hold me in his arms. Even if we didn't talk at times, he was there by my side. Now, with Tyshawn here, he... He doesn't do that. Maybe I'm just being over dramatic about it. Maybe I had gotten too attached to this man. Too use to his presence being around. Whatever the case was, I wasn't feeling it.

I felt myself drifting off to sleep. Alone and in silence without my Baby behind me to rock me to sleep.

Four Bullets

The next few days with Tyshawn was a task. He was the laziest, nastiest motherfucker I ever met. He would eat and wouldn't clean up after himself. After he would take a shower, or even use the bathroom at that, he would leave it a complete mess. Piss stained the side of the toilet and the floor, and I don't know how many times I've almost fallen into the toilet because he left the seat up. He also had this thing with the heater where, HE NEVER TURNED IT OFF. Burning up so much of our gas and Reese would let it slide.

All day, he would just eat and complain, eat and complain about a ton of different shit. Reese was getting fed up with it too. I could tell by his demeanor towards Tyshawn. They would begin to argue over simple things. For instance, yesterday, Reese asked him to simply clean up after himself when he was done eating. That turned into a whole disagreement where Tyshawn brought up old shit from their past.

His demeanor towards me was no different. He always seemed to be staring at me, making me feel so uncomfortable. He would say sly shit under his breath to me that ranged from hateful words, to how he wanted to be with me and how he was so much better than Reese. I never said anything to Reese about it. I just wanted to keep the peace between the two, but I was getting tired of it.

The situation between Reese and Tyshawn was also taking a toll on Reese and me. There were times where we would disagree about the actions of Tyshawn and not talk to each other for a while.

They would stay up at night talking and I was left alone to go to sleep by myself, night after night. A very uncomfortable sleep at that. We couldn't even be intimate how we wanted to because Tyshawn was ALWAYS THERE.

He had only been here for 6 days total and was already causing serious problems. In my opinion, this motha fucka had to go, but for some reason, Reese wouldn't kick him out. He said, he was like a brother to him when they were growing up. I asked myself, "Well, what the fuck changed?"

I awoke one morning from my slumber to find Reese's arm tightly wrapped around me. I smiled and rubbed it gently before getting up for my morning routine. I rubbed my eyes trying to finish waking up as I approached the bathroom. Before I could reach the door, it flung open, and I was left standing there in front of Tyshawn's half naked body.

I shielded my eyes and took a few steps back. "I'm sorry." I said, before moving back a little further so he could pass me.

I heard him smirk and approach me slowly. He grabbed my hands away from my face and put them on his body. "No need to be sorry."

I snatched my hands away from him and looked him dead in the eyes as I yelled, "What the fuck is wrong with you?"

He held his finger up to his lips and shushed me before he spoke. "I know you want this." he whispered. "I see the way you look at me." That same stark grin appeared on his face.

I looked at him in shock. "I don't fuckin want you. I want nothing to do with you." I barked and went into the bathroom, slamming and locking the door behind me.

I sat on the toilet lid for a while in disbelief that this had just happened. Soon, I heard Maureese's voice on the other side of the door. "What is going on?" he yelled.

"Nothing man, you know how women are. She wants her cake and eat it too." Tyshawn replied.

I stood up off the toilet and headed for the door as Maureese spoke. "What is that supposed to mean?" Before Tyshawn could respond, I flung open the door. "What the fuck is going on?" he yelled and looked me in my face.

"I came to the bathroom while he was coming out. He forced my hands on his body talkin about some, 'I know you want this.' and I snatched them away and yelled at him before going into the bathroom."

Reese turned and looked at Tyshawn with furry in his eyes. "That true bro?" he said, walking and getting in his face. Before Tyshawn could speak, Reese yelled, "Let's get one thing straight. This," he said, pointing to me, "is my girl. If you're going to be staying here, don't even THINK about it." He pushed his fingers into Tyshawn's temple. "Don't look at her, don't talk to her and don't even THINK about touching her. Got it?" he yelled.

Tyshawn nodded his head in submission. Reese let him go. "Come on bro, I would never do something like that to you. She came on to me."

"You're such a fuckin liar." I screamed as I went to punch him in his shit.

Reese got in the way and blocked my blow and said to Tyshawn, "You heard what the fuck I said. I will merk you if you touch her again. Or even look at her the wrong way."

"You got it man, you got it." he said, walking away from us.

Reese turned and looked at me and grabbed my face in his hands. "You ok Baby?"

I shook free of his grasps and walked away. "I'm fine." I heard him sigh from behind me as I went and sat back down on the bed.

I sat there with a blank stare on my face for a long time. Tyshawn's presence was really stressing me out.

Finally, I got up, put my boots on and headed towards the door. "Where are you going?" Reese asked, grabbing my arm.

"I'm going for a walk. I just… I just need some space." I looked at him with pleading eyes, hoping he would just let me walk out the door in peace.

He gave me a big hug. "Be careful. Don't go too far, and don't let the dark catch you." He opened the door and I proceeded out.

I walked through the woods with an attitude at first, but then, as I looked around at the trees and the scenery, I began to calm down. I found myself sitting on a large boulder just taking it all in. The cold air brushed past my wet skin, and I shivered.

About two hours had passed and I sat there on that rock just relaxing, enjoying the quiet. Enjoying my alone time away from Tyshawn. The only thing that would have made it better is if Reese was by my side enjoying it with me. I fumbled with the necklace around my neck as I thought about him.

I stood up and stretched and rubbed my sore cheeks. One last time, I looked around before walking back to the cabin. When I walked in through the door, both men were sitting in their respective chairs, and they looked frustrated and aggravated with each other.

I took a deep breath and began to take my boots off. The energy and the tension in the room was strong. "What's going on?" I asked. I walked over to Reese who was staring blankly into the kitchen and touched his shoulder gently. "What's going on?" I repeated.

He threw my hand off him. I looked at him confused. "You want him Natalie?"

I paused for a minute. "What?" I snapped angrily and confused.

"You been telling him how you want him behind my back?"

I shook my head as I looked from Reese to Tyshawn who had a devilish grin on his smug fucking face. "What the fuck did you tell him?" I yelled and tried to attack him.

Reese held me back. He looked deep into my eyes with disbelief and pain in them. "Did you?"

"Fuck no. It was the other way around. He wants to get with me. I only want to be with you." I yelled. My eyes teared up as I gently put my hand to his face.

"You fuckin lying bitch. You tell me all the time you wish Mar would leave so we could be alone together."

I looked at Tyshawn so confused. "I would never say that." I turned and looked at Reese again. "I would never say that. You don't actually believe that, do you?"

Reese shook his head. "I don't know. I don't know."

"What the fuck you mean you don't know? Are you serious right now, Maureese?" I stared at him trying to study him. He truly looked confused and didn't know what to think.

"If he was coming on to you Natalie, why wouldn't you say something to me about it?"

"Because I'm tired of the arguing and the yelling. Every DAY it's something new with this fucking guy. Every day he tries to draw a wedge between us and aggravate us. But for whatever reason, you won't kick him the fuck out. I don't get it." I stepped back from Maureese and looked at him in disbelief and disappointment. "But now I'm the bad guy? I can't believe you wouldn't trust and believe me over him."

"He's known me longer. Of course, he would trust me over a lying ass hoe like you." Tyshawn roared.

"Don't talk to me like that, you sorry sack of shit." I blurted.

"Don't talk to her like that bro." Reese said in my defense.

"She is a fuckin hoe bro. How she gone be here with you and den try n get with me. She barely knows either of us, yet she throwin pussy at the both of us."

180

I lunged at Tyshawn and swung. My fist connected with his jaw, and he went down. I didn't stop. I jumped on top of him and continued punching him dead in his shit until his face started leakin. Reese pulled me up off him and tried to hug me to calm me down.

I shoved him off of me and readjusted my hoodie with my shoulders. "You really gonna believe that punk ass over me? I don't give a fuck how long you've known each other. I would never do some shit like that." I said and watched as Tyshawn slowly rose to his feet with a smile.

"That's as close to me as you'll ever get baby girl. I don't want that stank ass pussy you slingin." He wiped his face and checked for blood. He looked surprised as he saw a lot of it coming from his face. He lunged towards me, and Reese punched him dead in his chest. He fell to the ground and gasped for air.

"Sit the fuck down bro. Don't you ever try and come at her like that." Reese stood over Tyshawn who slowly sat up.

He was torn in two. Conflicted on which one of us was telling the truth or not. "Reese, from day one this asshole has been coming on to me. Even earlier today he was tryna start with me. I can't believe you can't even see that."

I walked away from the both of them and went into the bathroom. The door slammed behind me before I let out a frustrated scream. Not only from the situation that was unfolding in front of me, but from the terrible stench of piss that was coming from the bathroom. It never smelled like this before that jackass came here. It felt like I was living in filth.

I couldn't believe that he was actually believing all his lies. After all we had been through. Even what he had seen with his own eyes from Tyshawn, and he was still taking his side. This was unbelievable. I sat there in shock. My hands throbbed from punching Tyshawn, and they shook from the anger I had steadily growing inside me. I shook them to relieve the pain.

I just sat there with my thoughts until the bathroom door opened. I looked up and saw Maureese standing there. I turned away from him and hung my head low. He didn't say anything for a while, just stood there watching me until I broke the silence.

"What do you want Maureese?" I asked in an aggravated tone.

He walked over to me and grabbed my hands pulling me up. He brought me to his chest where he held me there for a while. My tears, once again, soaked his hoodie.

He looked at my hands and ran cold water over them trying to get the swelling down. He gently dried them and pulled me into the main cabin area. It was quiet. I looked around and realized it was only us there. "I told him to go take a walk." he said, quietly.

I followed his lead as he brought me over to the bed and sat me down. He kept looking at me, but I couldn't even look back at him. Silence fell about the cabin as we both sat there for a while. Gathering our thoughts. Gathering the strength to talk about what needed to be discussed.

"I believe you Nat." he finally said to me. I still couldn't look him in the face. "You hear me?"

"I heard you Maureese." I took a deep breath in.

"I'm sorry."

I glared at him out the corner of my eyes. I still couldn't turn to look at him. I was so furious with him. "You're sorry? That's all you have to say is you're sorry?"

"Listen, when you left, he came to me on some man-to-man shit. He told me that every time I would leave the room, you would go over and flirt with him and tell him how you wanted to be with him and what not. With the past that we had together, I believed him at first. But knowing who you are and the connection that we have, I was skeptical about it. I was pissed off at what he told me. I care for you so much and his words were like knives in my chest."

I fumbled with my necklace as he spoke. I listened to his words and understood where he was coming from, but that didn't make a difference to me at the time and point.

He continued. "I know him being here hasn't been the easiest to deal with. It's stressing both of us out and quite frankly, I'm tired of the bullshit and the games he plays."

"So, what are you going to do about it?" I interrupted.

"He's gotta go. I've put so much stress on myself and you over these past couple of days, trying to do the right thing. Like I told you before, his cousin was like a brother to me. He gave me a roof over my head when I didn't have anywhere to go. He fed me, took care of me when no one else would. So, you can see why it's not that easy for me to just kick him out like that.

But after this? After this bullshit, he has to go. I can't take someone treating you this way or thinking I'm some kind of fool. Taking my kindness for weakness. Tomorrow, we're going to go on a nice long walk, but I'm the only one coming back. Alright?"

He took my hands in his and squoze them. "Ouch!" I said and flinched in pain.

"I'm sorry, I'm sorry, I forgot." He brought my hands up to his lips and kissed them. "Can you EVER forgive me Babe. I truly am sorry."

I finally looked up at him and all the sincerity in the world was on his face. I took another deep breath and nodded my head yes. "I forgive you Reese."

He wrapped his arms around me once again and gave me a big hug and I hugged him back.

The cabin door flung open, and Tyshawn came back in. He didn't take his boots off and left mud marks all throughout the room. "Come on bro, take your boots off." Reese shouted.

"It's cool bro. It's cool." He closed the door behind him and continued to walk through the cabin headed to the kitchen where he ransacked it like he owned everything in there. The food he took out was thrown carelessly on the counter. He acted like this was his home.

Finally, he sat down in his chair and began eating. I looked at the mess he left on the counter and on the floors I had just cleaned yesterday. My blood began to boil. I looked up at Maureese and his jaw was locked again as he watched Tyshawn's actions.

When he was done, he threw the wrapper to his food on the floor, stood up and shook the crumbs off his hoodie before sitting back down and resting. Reese stood up and walked over to where he was.

"So, is this bitch leaving or what?" Tyshawn said with a sense of security and confidence.

"No. She's not leaving, but you are." Reese said as he gripped him up by his collar and began dragging him to the door.

"Aye man, what the fuck is you doin?" Tyshawn yelled as he tried to fight back with Maureese. I covered my mouth as I sat there and watched in shock as the scene unfolded in front of me.

Reese finally let him go when they were in front of Tyshawn's clothes. "Pack your shit up. You can't stay here anymore."

"Stop fuckin with me? You serious? You kicking me out after what I just told you about her?"

"Get your shit and get the fuck out. I'm not dealing with this anymore."

Tyshawn stood up big and got into Reese's face. Reese got big back and stood his ground. "I'm not going anywhere. She is." Tyshawn said and turned to me and began heading my way.

I jumped up to my feet and ran away from him before he could get to me. Reese grabbed him back and slung him to the floor, but Tyshawn had a grip on him, so when he fell, so did Maureese. They began wrestling and fighting on the floor. It all happened so fast, I couldn't wrap my mind around it.

It seemed like it was a fight for life and death as blow after blow was taken and given by both men. I stood there frozen, watching everything that was happening until Reese got on top and started punching him ferociously.

I stepped in and tried to pull Reese off him but ended up getting hit in the process. My face seared with pain, and I held it as Reese continued to punch him until he stopped. Out of breath, he stood up and looked down at Tyshawn who was barely moving.

He looked up at me with a look on his face I had never seen before. His eyes were glazed over, his face was covered in blood, but not all his. He began to walk towards me, and I took a few steps back. I was scared of him. His face changed back to normal as he came up to me and looked at where he had hit me.

He grabbed me and held me stroking my hair gently when out of nowhere, his body went limp, and fell to the floor almost taking me down with him. I stood there stunned, not knowing what happened until I looked down and saw the knife sticking out of his back. And now, Tyshawn was coming after me.

I ran over to our gun bags and fumbled about in them, but he was on me and pulled me to the ground and began hitting me in the face. I felt his weight come off me as Reese grabbed him and started fighting with him again. I heard Reese yell out in pain as Tyshawn took the knife out of his back and stabbed him. Once, twice, three times.

I grabbed my gun from the bag and cocked it back. I pulled the trigger, but nothing happened. The sound of the trigger caused Tyshawn to look my way and he began to come at me once again. I took the safety off and pulled the trigger and his body dropped to the floor. I walked up to him and pulled the trigger four more times, putting four bullets in his chest to ensure he wasn't getting back up.

I put the gun down and ran over to where Maureese's lifeless body was. There was so much blood. So, so, so much blood everywhere. I went and got the first aid kit and towels and applied pressure to his wounds. I checked his pulse. It was very faint.

"Reese!" I yelled in pure agony and fear. "Reese!" I yelled again. I began to cry. I didn't know what to do.

I took a deep breath and tried to concentrate on what needed to be done. My negative thoughts interfered with my concentration until I brushed them out altogether.

I took off his shirt and analyzed what was going on. I had no idea what I was doing. What if he had internal bleeding? How could I fix that? I applied pressure to the stab wounds with one hand while I fumbled around in the first aid kit for sutures. My shaking hands made it difficult to thread the needle.

I took another deep breath and calmed my nerves so that I could do what I needed to do. Alcohol was poured on his wounds before I began to sew him up. He yelled and sat straight up.

"Shh. Shh. Shh. Baby. Lay back. Lay back. It's ok."

"What's going on?" he yelled. His voice was stricken with pain and fear. "Babe?" he asked looking up at me.

"I'm right here Baby. I'm right here. You gotta relax." I tried to calm him down.

"What's going on?" He put his hand on his wounds and looked at all the blood that was coming out of him. "What the fuck! What the fuck!" he repeated and laid his head back down under the guidance of my hands.

"Hold this right here. Put pressure on it." I demanded. He did as I asked. "You have to be still ok? Stay awake. I need you ok?"

He nodded his head, but his breathing was erratic. "I need you to breathe." I put my bloody hands on his face so he could focus on me and my breathing instead of the pain. "Breathe. Watch me. Breathe." His eyes focused on me, and he began to calm down. "I have to sew this up ok." He nodded his head at my words and laid back.

Tears streamed down my face at his agony. I took the needle and thread in my hands once again, sanitized it and began sewing up his cuts. He yelled out in pain again. "Baby, be still. You have to be still."

"Ok." he uttered.

"Take a deep breath and be still." He did as I asked again, and I continued stitching him up. I cut the thread and began on the next wound. He tried so hard not to flinch as I sewed him back together.

"There's one more on this side." I said to him. "Ready?"

"Go!" he shouted, and I began stitching up the last wound. I poured alcohol on them again and he yelled. "Babe, WHAT THE FUCK!"

"I know, I know, I'm so sorry."

"What the FUCK!" he yelled again.

Clean gauze was applied before I took a deep breath to try and calm my nerves once more. I looked him in the eyes. "I have to roll you over."

"What?"

"I have to sew up the last one."

"I thought that was the last one." he yelled hysterically.

I shook my head. "There's one more on your back."

He mustered up the strength and turned over on his side while I prepared the last sutures.

His breathing was still fast as I asked, "Are you ready?"

"Go Babe. Just get it over with!" he yelled at me.

Once again, I sanitized the wound with alcohol, and he yelled out. The sutures were sterilized, and I began to sew him up again. I put the clean gauze on like I did the ones in the front.

When I was done, the room was quiet. Too Quiet. I went around to the front and looked at him. He wasn't moving. "Reese?!" I yelled and shook him a bit. "Reese?!" I yelled again and got no response. I felt for a pulse, but one wasn't there. I began to panic.

I rolled him on his back and began CPR. Over and over again I performed. In between, I stopped to check for his pulse. Nothing. I laid on his chest and cried. "Wake up!" I yelled. "Wake the fuck up!" I hollered.

In my anger and frustration, I began to hit his chest. "Wake the fuck up! I'm sorry." I repeated. I began CPR again, not wanting to give up on him. Until finally, I got a very weak pulse back.

My tears stopped flowing from my face as I held my breath and continued to feel his pulse. I laid down on his chest and listened intently to his faint heartbeat.

I stood to my feet and pulled his heavy ass out of the pool of blood. A few blankets were laid out on the floor, and I rolled him on top of them and put a pillow behind his head.

His body temperature was cold, so the heater was turned on and brought over to him. Several blankets were thrown on top to help try and raise his temperature back up. I checked his pulse once more and it was still there.

I looked around at the cabin which was covered in blood. Pools of it was on the floor. The walls were splattered and smeared with it. I looked at Tyshawn's lifeless body and kicked it. "You. Son. Of. A. Bitch." I yelled with every kick I gave. His lifeless eyes stared up at me. A bullet hole was square in the middle of his forehead.

I grabbed his arms and drug him to the front of the cabin where I opened the doors and rolled his body out. I grabbed his legs and drug him deep into the woods. I spit on him before I walked away, leaving him there to rot.

I returned to the cabin and checked on Reese. His heartbeat was still there, but his breathing was shallow. What I did wasn't going to be enough.

I looked about the cabin again and began to clean it up. Wiped the walls down, mopped up all the blood and organized everything back in its place. Blood-stained clothes and towels were tossed into the machine with some water so they could soak for a while.

In the bathroom, I looked at my unrecognizable and swollen face. My attention turned to my hands. My murderous, lifesaving hands. I turned the water on and washed all the blood away. The tears never seemed to stop as I did so. I couldn't believe I killed someone and saved someone in the same hour. Did I feel bad that I took someone's life? Absolutely. Did I regret it? Absolutely not.

I took a shower and washed off all the blood, pain and horror from the night. I even had to wash the blood out of my hair.

I got dressed, cleaned up the bathroom and checked on Reese again. He was in the same condition I had left him in. I checked his stomach for any bloating or inflammation. So far, there wasn't any.

Tears continuously poured out of my eyes as I cleaned him up. His face was wiped free of the blood and the rest of his wounds were attended to. After he was wiped down fully, clean clothes were put on him ever so carefully. I sat next to him quietly. Holding his hand and hoping that he would be ok.

My mind kept wandering. I was so tired, yet the adrenaline wouldn't let me slow down. There was nothing left for me to do but sit and watch over him. Making sure he was doing alright. I watched him. Fighting for his life. I watched him and was helpless.

My head came down on his chest as it had done every single night since we met. His heartbeat sang a new tune.

More to Come

Be sure to keep an eye out for the next book in the series, '*The Hunted: The Worst Has Just Begun*'.

Find out if Maureese survives or are his wounds too great for him to survive? How will Natalie go on without him?

About the Author

Leaza Norman is from South Carolina but moved to New Jersey and has been there ever since. As early as 2001 she has been writing short stories, poems and lyrics that have eventually led her to writing novels. The first of which is *The Hunted: How It Started*. Being a hopeless romantic herself, most of the novels and other works she has written have been around love and romance. Most of the characters are put into difficult and even non-traditional situations and must battle with their heart to prevail in the end.

www.ingramcontent.com/pod-product-compliance
Lightning Source LLC
Chambersburg PA
CBHW022152240626
47153CB00007B/2624